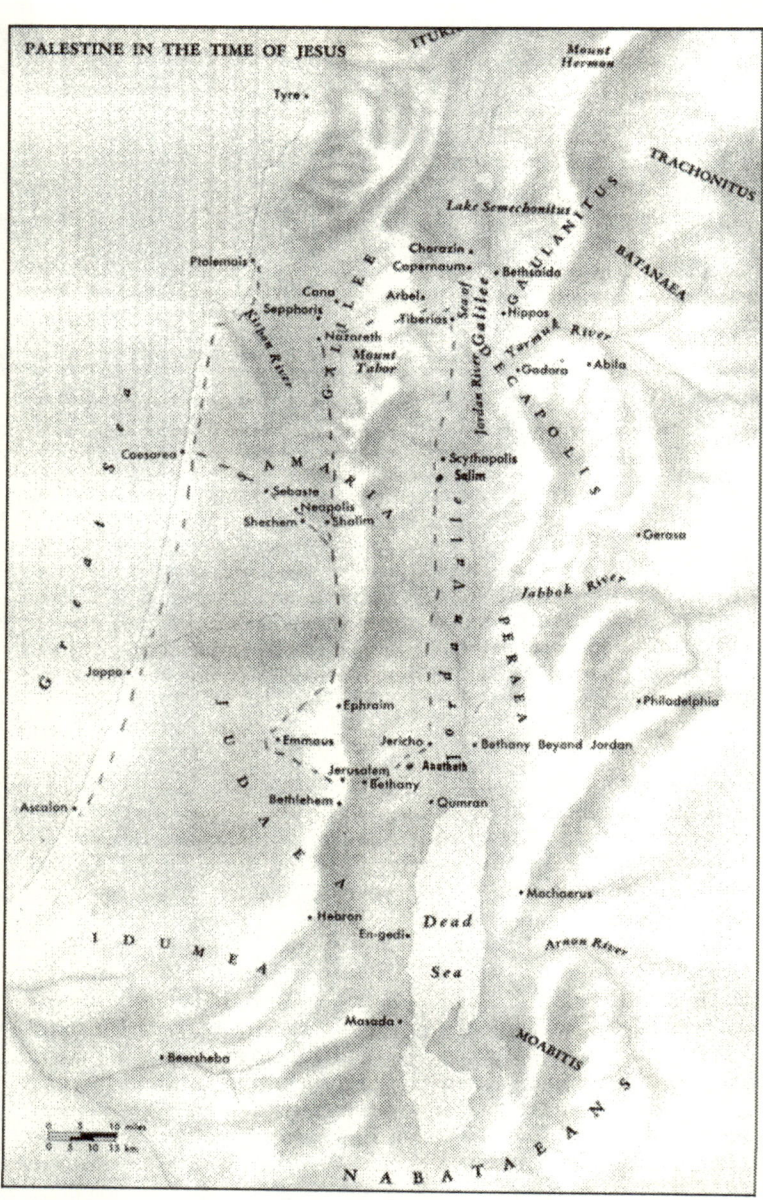

PALESTINE IN THE TIME OF JESUS

ITUR...
Mount Herman

Tyre

TRACHONITUS

Lake Semechonitus

BATANAEA

GAULANITUS

Charazin
Capernaum
Bethsaida

Ptolemais

Cana
Sepphoris

Arbel
Tiberias

Sea of Galilee

Hippos

Yarmuk River

Nazareth

Jordan River

DECAPOLIS

Mount Tabor

Gadara

Abila

Nahum River

GALILEE

Caesarea

SAMARIA

Scythapolis
Salim

Sebaste
Neapolis
Shechem
Shalim

Gerasa

Jabbok River

JUDAEA

PERAEA

Jappa

Ephraim

Philadelphia

Emmaus
Jerusalem
Bethlehem

Jericho
Anathoth
Bethany

Bethany Beyond Jordan

Ascalon

Qumran

IDUMEA

Hebron
En-gedi

Machaerus

Dead

Sea

Arnon River

Masada

MOABITIS

Beersheba

NABATAEANS

0   5   10 miles
0 5 10 15 km.

The Carpenter's Apprentice

Matthew Price

Americana Publishing, Inc.
303 San Mateo Boulevard NE
Albuquerque, New Mexico 87108-1382 USA
(888) 883-8203
www.americanabooks.com

ISBN: 1-58943-066-2

Library of Congress Control Number: 2004118372

Acknowledgements

I would first like to thank the living Jesus Christ. Without His small, still voice and inspiring direction, I would still be trying to write a parenting book.

Thanks to my wife, Lenore, for enduring the far-off looks of a writer in another time and place and for giving up some of her time with me.

All authors have their first editor and so, many thanks to Pat Woods, who took pity on this writer and braved a three-foot slush pile in return for a pastor's prayer. Enjoy seminary, Pat.

Thank you, Ted, for keeping this book alive and never giving up hope. Who would have ever thought that a fictional book about Jesus would be edited and championed by a Jew and published by a secular publisher that specializes in truck stop audio books?

Many thanks to my friends in Great Bend, Kansas. To Jennifer Schartz and Chuck Smith, who decided that – with a little help – I could write stories that people would like to hear. To Linda and Stacey, thanks for your friendship and for covering for me when I was writing this book instead of paginating.

Thank you, Mom, for being my biggest fan and encouraging me and for reassuring me that I wasn't committing heresy by writing this book.

A special thanks to the people of First Southern Baptist Church of Claflin and Trinity Baptist Church of Benkelman, for permitting me and encouraging me in writing my columns and books.

Finally, thank you Dorey and Jennifer, for the prayers needed to move the hand of God.

Prelude

The three men stumbled into the village looking barely alive and looking even less like human beings. The legionnaires driving them were bored with the job of guarding and driving them and flicked the whip across their charges' back, almost as an after-thought and for lack of something else to do. The dust kicked up by the stumbling men gave both Roman legionnaire and prisoner a sharpened thirst for the water they were stopping for.

The soldiers looked around the small little town and saw not a soul on the narrow rock-paved street. They would have been surprised if they had seen anybody. It was Saturday and, as this was a predominantly Jewish town, all of the businesses were shut down for the Sabbath save for the Roman inn and tavern that were always open.

The group of soldiers and prisoners stopped at the small town's cistern well, in front of what looked like a small temple or some other kind of religious place, for a refreshing drink of water. They were on their way with the prisoners to Caesarea, the capitol of the northern part of Palestine, where the men were to be tried and executed. That they would be found guilty was a foregone conclusion.

The chained men had been caught robbing a caravan down south in Samaria, the central mountainous region of Palestine, a few weeks back, and there was only one punishment for that kind of crime. The soldiers of the detail thought the ultimate punishment would be especially fitting for one of the thieves. The prisoner named Thaddeus had fought, killed and injured fellow legionnaires at the time of his capture and the harsh punishments that the Roman

Empire was known for were meant to discourage that kind of behavior.

The soldiers drank their fill while the prisoners waited on their knees, with no protection from the midday sun. After the legionnaires were done the three men rose to their feet and stumbled up to the well where they again fell to their knees.

Each man had a large crossbeam across the back of his neck, behind his head. The hands were tied around the wooden beam, which weighed approximately fifty pounds. There were no shackles on their ankles for indeed if any of them made a run for it they would only get as far as the throw of a Roman javelin or stumble over the first rock they encountered. The action would only lead to more severe beatings and the men just wanted some peace for their last few days.

The three men plunged their faces into the cistern well that collected any rain that fell in the arid region and stored it for the various life-sustaining purposes of the village. Mazer, the captain of this guard detail, walked up behind the three prisoners, already refreshed by his own drink of water and from the skin of wine he carried. With a demonic look of pure glee, he began to savagely beat his weary and thirsty charges with a three-pronged whip, each of the ends having a small lead ball wrapped in leather. The weighted straps left fresh welt marks on two of the wretched men's backs. With a particularly vicious swing, Mazer drew thin lines of blood on the other.

Thaddeus, a native Samaritan whose back was a bleeding mess, could take no more. He had joined the roving band of thieves in the Samarian Mountains over two years before. Now to be humiliated like this in a predominately

Jewish town, in front of what was obviously the town's synagogue, was beyond what he could endure. He had hoped that one of the soldiers would have killed him right then and there for the fight he had put up back in the mountains at the time of his capture. The one thing he had not wanted and had tried to avoid by his defiance was to be treated like an animal at the hands of the cruel Romans who ruled the world.

He continued to drink from the well while bringing his feet up under him, even as he was beaten by the sadistic Mazer, who he cursed and thanked in his mind for bringing him to this decision. In a lighting fast move, Thaddeus jumped straight back into Mazer, sending the cross beam attached to his shoulders under the chin of the Roman centurion. The sudden action sent the soldier flying backward where he hit the ground with blood gushing from all orifices of his head. The story would be told and retold in the weeks to come and the flight of the Roman centurion would get longer and higher with each retelling.

Thaddeus dove headfirst into the cistern well, crossbeam and all, after hitting the Roman beating him and before the other soldiers of the detail could react. They had been sitting under a sycamore tree waiting for the prisoners to finish drinking. The condemned man sank like a millstone to the bottom of the well that was over ten feet deep. His last dying thought before he allowed the water to be sucked into his lungs was that he hoped he had broken the jaw of the cruel soldier, who would beat a man while taking a drink of water.

The thought occurred to him that the town's people would lose all the water of the well until they could pull his body out. The thought pleased the dying Samaritan because he knew the people who used the well thought his people to be half-human. They would either have to wait for the rain to refill it or lug water up from the stream he had seen outside the town's gates. Thaddeus died with a smile of contempt for a world where there was no hope of a better life for people like him.

The other two prisoners were quickly chained to the nearest post while the legionnaires tried to fish the captive out of the well. When a large meat hook was finally used to drag the bottom of the cistern, it caught the dead Thaddeus behind the neck and ten of the soldiers lifted him out of his watery grave. Mazer had gone off to the Roman inn to wait for the local physician, who would be summoned after the sun went down and the doctor's Sabbath was over. Mazer's jaw was indeed broken, in two places no less, and his nose was also bent at an impossible angle. The odds going around the troop were that the captain would probably not be heard from for a long time. His men last caught a glance of the hurt man as he walked away toward the inn, squinting at the pain while holding his cloak to his face.

The second in command sent a runner on to Sepphoris for instructions. In the meantime, the soldiers moved to a spot just outside the gates of the small town of Nazareth and set up camp for the night. The officers that were left would join their captain at the inn, but the common soldiers of the detachment would have to rough it beside the road. Mazer's second-in-command knew that he would get word back from the garrison as to what should be done with the ailing centurion and also with the remaining prisoners by the next morning. He was contented to wait for such instruction in the tavern and inn, where the beverages were tastier and beds softer than what his men would have outside of town. Rank did have its privileges.

On Sunday morning, the soldier that had been sent out came back with the detail's new orders and instructions.

Since the robbers were causing trouble and no more trouble was needed in Galilee, the region ruled by Herod the Tetrarch, the prisoners were to be executed there, in Nazareth. The legion commander's signature was on the proclamation that said the remaining two prisoners had received a fair trial and were found guilty. The punishment would be crucifixion until death and the sentence was to be carried out immediately.

The new escort leader nodded his approval after reading the orders, and with a long sigh, sent his men out to find big enough trees that could accommodate the executions. He would have helped them but it was not right for the leader to be seen working alongside the common soldiers and besides, his head was hurting from too much drink from the night before.

Sunday afternoon the crowd of curious town's folk gathered at the gates of the small city as the two remaining thieves were hoisted high in the air. The beam that each man carried had been attached to the larger polls that had been crudely cut from the trees found early that day. The poles had then been lifted up into the air and the bottoms of the poles were slid into holes dug for just this purpose.

The town's men stood around their nightly council fire that was just inside the gates of the city and tried not to pay any attention to what was going on outside of the town limits. No one had been crucified in Nazareth since the town had became a town and parents kept their children inside and away from the horror show that was taking place just outside the gates.

The town's carpenter had been raided for some of the supplies needed to carry out the executions. The man silently obeyed the soldiers who had asked for the pegs, hammers, saws and planes. He was sick that something like this was being done in his small town. Lining the roads to large towns throughout Palestine or any other country that Rome held in sway, one could see crosses as a regular course of matter; however the small towns were usually left alone. This was apparently an unusual case.

Most of those that looked on were the younger men. They had not seen enough death and butchery to know that such things were not worth their attention. They gathered in curious groups of twos and threes to watch the spectacle. They would stare in fascination for as long as it took them to hear the men cry out in pain or hear a joint or a bone give before they retreated to the fire with the older men. Soon all of the townsfolk left the men to die alone. They abandoned the condemned men by turning their backs and walking away, ending their nightly meeting early.

Crucified men died multiple deaths all at the same time. Because their hands are tied and sometimes nailed to the cross beam that is suspended above their heads, they find it hard to breath and have to lift up in order to take a breath. That action puts horrible pressure on the muscles. The weight of their entire body drags down, causing joints of the elbows and shoulders to pop out of place. Blood and liquid eventually start to fill the lungs of those hanging and the crucified man or woman starts to drown.

The strong were at a disadvantage when it came to dying on a cross. The weak died quickly; usually by suffocation after their muscles ceased to be able to lift them for the breath needed to sustain life. The strong and young were able to endure for a much longer time and therefore increased their agony. Sometimes the Roman in charge of the crucifixion took pity on the condemned and with a heavy lead bar broke the bones of the legs. Mercifully death came swiftly after that.

The two crucified thieves outside the gates of Nazareth were still alive after five hours of hanging and because of the complete darkness that surrounded them as the night wore on, they were terrified and lonely. Their hands and feet were tied to the wooden poles and not pierced through, so blood loss was not a factor in their dying. Still, the men were in their final throes of pure agony as their muscles spasmed and their lungs burned from lack of oxygen.

The legionnaires who were charged with carrying out the sentence were not obliged to stand and watch. They headed off to the tavern for traveling men such as themselves. Most of them had seen too much death and dying in their own time. The dying, they told each other, could keep each other company, they would return in the morning to bury what was left.

While the people of the town tried to carry on as if everything was normal, one boy could not pretend to act that way. He had never told a lie. He couldn't pretend that those men dying on the outskirts of the town he grew up in didn't exist. That would have been a monstrous lie.

He slipped out of his house and went to the city gates, without even informing his mother. His father would not see him as the man had already come back from the nightly fire.

The young boy approached the two thieves as they hung on their respective crosses. He could see the anguish and pain in the faces of the pair suffering the most horrible death known to man. Out of compassion, the boy picked up a long stick and tore a piece of cloth from the bottom of his tunic. He hurried to the stream that ran along side the village and wet the cloth. He then ran back to the crosses and lifted up the stick and let the men suck some moisture from the cloth.

The boy felt that he should say a prayer for the two of them. They had not said a word of acknowledgement for the kind deed of the young man, so lost were they in their own pain. The boy took one more look at the spectacle and bowed his head. "Oh God, keep me from dying such a death as this," the boy asked with tears in his eyes. Then as always, he surrendered to the will of his Creator and prayed, "Nevertheless, let Your will be done instead of mine."

One

Destructive Anger

Everyone heard the ram's-horn's distinctive tone that Monday afternoon in the small town of Nazareth. The unique sound was especially sweet to the students of the village rabbinical school. The children, considered young adult men by the tenets of the Jewish faith they studied under the care of Rabbi Moshe, anxiously looked up at the middle-aged teacher for the nod that would release them from another day's learning.

Moshe was not known for his dynamic speaking and teaching ability, but had been a rather mediocre student under an all but forgotten rabbi in Jerusalem years before. He had been posted years before in the northern Galilean city because a local replacement for his predecessor could not be found and no other rabbi from Judea in the south had wanted to be stigmatized with the assignment.

While the men and elders of the small town trusted the Judean born rabbi because he was good of character and morals and was not given to strong drink, it was common knowledge among the townsfolk that none of their boys would excel in the Torah if they left the education solely in the less than brilliant rabbi's hands.

"I want each of you boys to think about your lessons," said the rabbi. "And remember that the well out front is still unclean — do not drink from it." Moshe indicated with the lazy toss of his hand that class was dismissed.

The boys erupted to their feet from the spots on the hard dirt floor where moments before they had been seated in front of a raised platform. Looking like a puppeteer had pulled each of the teen-age boys up off the floor, they started fast to the door, each trying to beat the other out the door and be the first to breathe the fresh air of freedom for at least a week.

This was to be the last class for almost a week. The planting season was upon the small village and the boys' fathers would need all the help they could get from the time the sun rose until it set. Most of the town's men and boys were expected to show up to help during planting and harvest seasons. In fact, every Jewish family that had lived in Nazareth for longer than seven years owned their own piece of land.

Since the time of General Joshua, successor to Moses the Lawgiver, and the initial conquering of the land of Canaan, each of the twelve tribes of Israel was allotted its own parcel in the land. Within that parcel, the land was broken up to individual families as an inheritance forever. Land could be sold or borrowed on, but every fifty years, the land would go back to the surviving members of the original family.

Because of the deportations of the Jews by Syria, Assyria, and Babylon by Sennacherib and Nebuchadnezzar over 400 years in the past; each family lost the land that had been given to them at the time the land had been conquered. Only land in the southern part of Palestine had been reallocated after the Jews came back from Babylon, in the times of the scribe Ezra and the prophet Nehemiah.

The town of Nazareth was, in relation to its neighbors, a relatively new concern in the northern half of Palestine. The entire land had been fought over, almost as an afterthought, by every major dynasty from the Medes and Persians to the Greeks and finally the Romans. About forty years before, when King Herod the Great had come to power to govern the area for Rome, he had all but forced some Jews to emigrate to the north. The king's intention had been to move some of the people he ruled to settle and farm some of the rich farmland and then have it added to his kingdom by Rome. While this worked fine for Herod the Great in his lifetime, the kingdom didn't last long when it came time for his children to ascend his throne.

After he died, Rome split Herod the Great's kingdom into three tetrarchs or sub-kingdoms and appointed three of the king's children to rule over them. Knowing the traditions of the Jews and knowing why no one wanted to move north, Herod had promised anyone who would move their own plot of land. It didn't matter if a person was a town blacksmith, carpenter or moneylender; each would have his own farm to tend in addition to any other work they may have done.

While some liked the thought of a new start, for the most part the people who left for the north were poor and disenfranchised Jews. These were men and women who had sold or lost their family holdings. Many were displaced by the Roman occupation and many wanted to flee from the very benefactor who was offering the land.

Ten years earlier, that diseased and paranoid monarch had ordered slain every male child two years of age and younger in the entire southern half of his kingdom. The exodus from Judea to the north was especially heavy during that last year of the demented king's life.

The planted and seeded towns that were spread throughout the northern Tetrarchy survived only because the people were hardy and hard working. No aid came from the more prosperous south. Most of the men who lived in the town of Nazareth worked at two jobs. One job was so they and their families could eat and the other job was to make enough money from each other and passing travelers to buy such things that could be called comforts. Such as it was, everyone helped in the fields. The land was theirs and even though the rulers of Rome, Caesarea, and Jerusalem taxed them heavily, the people of the town called it home and they were willing to work hard to keep what they had.

A person didn't have to be a farmer; however, to know that without the produce and wheat that would come from the crops no one in the town would eat. Some of the town's old men and women had been through famines caused by inclement weather or acts of God and, from the stories they told, most of the younger generation was more than happy to put aside their regular routine and studies to go help in the fields.

Moshe was tired. His back ached and his head felt worse. The boys, at times, were almost too much for him to handle with their roughhousing, laughter, and loud conversation. Knowing that they were just being normal boys was of no solace to the headmaster and rabbi. He had wanted to be a scribe when he was younger; a profession that required no interaction with the general public and children, but his hand had proved too weak to copy the pages upon pages of script and scripture that were required of that profession.

He held his mangled right hand in front of his eyes. "May the ox that crushed you burn in hell," he cursed under his breath, remembering the day the beast had crushed three of his five fingers when he was five-years-old. He had been helping his father plow a field when he had tripped under the beast that pulled it. It was all he could do now to hold a writing quill in his hand. The pain, which had been a constant throb that matched his heart beat for most of his life to the point of his not noticing it, would become unbearable the moment he did more than sign his name.

He rolled up the scroll that had provided that day's lesson in the writings of the prophet Ezekiel. When he had rolled the two ends of the scroll together, he stood and walked to the rear of the platform that he sat upon while teaching the lessons. There, against the back wall was the chest that held the small town's copies of the Law and Prophets, also known as the Torah. The chest also held copies of the writings, opinions and commentaries of some of the most revered rabbis the Jewish faith and people had known.

As he reached the chest, Moshe became angry with himself and the station in life where he was seemingly stuck. "I should be copying these scrolls, not teaching snotty-nosed boys and their ignorant parents from them," he thought bitterly, not for the first time. His hand started aching from the simple act of just rolling the scroll – in sympathy, it seemed, with the very mental attention paid to it.

An impulsive rage seized Moshe and he lifted the writings of Ezekiel above his head with both hands and threw them down into the chest. At the very moment the scroll landed, a sound like a distressed peacock was heard throughout the two-story building, wailing and moaning. The whole piece of furniture burst into pieces and the scrolls spilled out on the floor, as if the wood of the chest was offended by the irreverent treatment of the scroll. Some of the scrolls rolled to the edge of the platform and fell into the students' court below.

Drawing in his breath and throwing his hands up over his head, the rabbi stared at his handiwork in disbelief and horror. Moshe collapsed to the ground sobbing, crying. "Oh Lord, what have I done? Oh God, please forgive me for being angry with you and causing the destruction of your precious words." The man was aghast at seeing the precious scrolls scattered on the floor.

The rabbi rose from the floor and went to the water basin to wash his face. It seemed to him he had been groveling and praying on the floor for more than an hour, but it was in fact only 10 minutes. He picked up the precious scrolls and piled them in a corner wearing a dejected and haunted look on his face. He then fled to his house and went directly to his bedchamber, to sulk and bemoan his human frailties.

His wife did not know how to console him. "You must eat, Moshe," she said. "The Lord will show you how He wants you to make this right." She kissed him and rubbed his neck as she tried to comfort him. "Just leave me alone," Moshe said as he squirmed beneath her touch. "I would not be surprised if God struck me dead for what I have done. When the town elders hear of my fit, they will ask Jerusalem to send another rabbi. I am ruined in front of my God and man." That night, Moshe lay in his bed and wept. He was both sorry for what he had done and angry with himself. "Oh my God, please show me how I can make this right," he prayed with all his might. "Lord please help me to be content with who I am and with what I do. Oh Lord, take this horrible, destructive anger away from me."

The answer, it seemed, came to him from out of nowhere. He would have the Torah chest rebuilt and he would dedicate his life to preserving both the scrolls and the chest that held them.

Moshe prayed one last prayer before he fell asleep. "Lord I promise you that I will commission the building of a new chest first thing in the morning. I also promise that I will do a better job with the children and that I will give more attention to their education. Lord help me to make up for my outburst against you and I will do anything you ask of me." With his promises made, peace flooded over the rabbi. Feeling the relief that only comes with confession, he fell asleep without saying the obligatory "amen."

Two

First Job

Joseph was busy with what seemed like the weight of the world on his shoulders. Old Joshua had checked in that morning almost as soon as the town's only carpenter had opened up for business. "Hello, Joseph. Peace be upon you and your house. Is the table I ordered almost done?" asked Joshua. "When can I expect to take delivery?"

"Hello, my friend. I am just putting the finishing touches on it now in the back work room," Joseph assured the town elder. "I will deliver your table to you this afternoon, if that is alright with you?"

"So it will be done on time then?" exclaimed Joshua. "Oh, Joseph, I should not have doubted you. Since I am here, may I take a look at what you have done so far?" Shoeing the town elder away, Joseph walked with Joshua to the door. "I never show a client the unfinished product, Joshua." Joseph said. "You will see it soon enough this afternoon when I sit it in your dinning area."

Joseph walked back into his workshop and was just picking up a tool when another voice called out his name. "Joseph? Joseph, are you here?"

Putting down his chisel with a loud sigh, Joseph got up to see who this new intruder was. "Hello, Naomi," Joseph said as he came into the front room of his workshop. Joseph noticed the careworn look on the widow's face and felt a sudden compassion for the woman who was forced to raise her family without the father.

"I need you to come and look at my front door," said the widow, who then bit her lip in embarrassment. "Last night my son came home in a drunken stupor, again, and he slammed the door as he shut it. The noise it made must have awakened everyone in the neighborhood. Anyway, this morning I went to go out my front door with my pitcher to the stream for the daily water and I could not get the door to close," Naomi explained. "I noticed that the door has come off its hinges and now it will not shut either right or tight."

Joseph had noticed the boy the night before, wandering off after the nightly council fire with old Tobias. The old man hadn't had a sober day or night in over 10 years. Tobias had been one of the refugees 10 years before who had come to the northern town to forget his troubles. When extremely drunk, the broken man would cry about losing both his son and his wife to the same soldier who was carrying out the bloody wishes of Herod. Tobias now only worked hard enough to pay for his next night of drinking. The house he lived in was ramshackle, unkempt, and unclean and his body smelled worse than the building he lived in.

Joseph had thought it strange at the time that one so young would run with an old drunk like Tobias, but now the carpenter suspected that it was the alcohol that drew the two of them together. "I will come by this afternoon and examine the door," Joseph told Naomi. "It may be that it can be fixed without replacing the whole door."

"Thank you, Joseph," said Naomi, who then turned to go. "I need to fetch the water. I will see you this afternoon. May God continue to grace your house with His peace."

Joseph returned to the three-section table feeling more rushed than normal. He only lacked the twelve legs being attached before he could consider the table finished. One thing or another had kept him from finishing this table in the time that he had quoted to old Joshua and now, if he didn't get it done, he would have to charge less than what he had quoted to the town elder.

Ten minutes later, Joseph threw down his hammer and chisel and put his head in his hands. He had just started the process of attaching the second of the twelve short legs to one of the sections of the table when he heard the dreaded sound. "Joseph?" cried the voice. "Joseph, are you here?"

Joseph thought he recognized the voice but picked up his tools and continued to work, pretending mostly to himself that he hadn't heard a sound. When the town's rabbi barged into the carpenter's workshop looking distraught and dismayed without even asking for permission to enter, Joseph's suspicions on the voice's owner were proved correct.

"Oh, Joseph, there you are," said Moshe out of breath. "You must not have heard me call out your name. I need you to build a new chest for the scrolls, the other one broke yesterday and now I need a new one right away. When can I have it done?" asked the rabbi who was talking so fast he ran out of air.

"Calm down, Moshe," said Joseph, as he led him out of his back workroom and seated him in a chair. "Let me pour you some wine before you pass out." The carpenter picked up a jug of sweet red wine that he kept for consummating business deals and poured the distraught rabbi a healthy belt, despite the early hour. "Now tell me what is wrong and what you need," asked Joseph who had managed to calm the excited rabbi.

"I need you to build a new chest for the Scripture scrolls," explained a calmer and slower talking Moshe. "The other one broke yesterday and now I need a new one just as soon as you can build it. When can I have it done?"

"Wait a minute," said Joseph. "What happened to the old one? It seemed fine this past Sabbath when I saw it."

"As I was placing the scroll I was teaching from yesterday," explained a suddenly nervous Moshe. "The whole box just crumbled in front of my eyes. The wood just groaned and then burst apart."

"That is strange," replied Joseph who suspected there might be more to the story than just that but held his piece.

"So how soon can a new one be built?" asked the eager rabbi, trying to pin Joseph into setting a time. "You always bring your jobs in on schedule."

"I can probably do it the first of next week," said Joseph. "I'm up to my ears in work at the moment."

"School will be back in session next week," argued the rabbi. "Besides, I don't want to have the Scriptures stacked on the floor. It's disrespectful to them."

Joseph let out a sigh and looked heavenward for patience and more time. "I didn't say I wouldn't do the job, Moshe," said Joseph. "If I bump the other jobs to do yours, my other customers will take their business elsewhere."

"Come on, Joseph," said Moshe, who was not going to be put off and looked like he was digging his feet in for a protracted argument. "No one will blame you for working on a project for the town's synagogue. This is for God," tried

Moshe, who was feeling the guilt of hastening the death of the old chest

"I don't know," said Joseph, who just wanted to get back to the table.

"I'll pay double if you can have the job done in a week," offered the guilt stricken rabbi. Joseph considered the rabbi before him and was about to tell him of the impossible situation he found himself in when the door of the shop opened once more. In strode Joseph's oldest son, Jesus, who would soon be twelve years of age. He had an earnest and inquisitive look on his face. Jesus pulled up short when he saw the rabbi, not wanting to disturb the business meeting that was clearly in progress between his father and the town cleric.

The boy was of average height, no more that 5' 2" and weighed no more than 100 pounds. He sported a medium build that already showed the promise of a muscled adult frame. He was crowned with curly brown hair that cascaded in rings down to his shoulders. Like most Jewish boys his age, a razor hardly ever found its way to his face and peach fuzz was starting to shadow the chin and jaw-line of the boy's face.

Jesus raised one of his thick brown eyebrows – a talent that always amazed his father – to Joseph as he stood to the side of where Moshe was sitting. Always inquisitive, he seldom interrupted a conversation, but, most times, would wait patiently for a pause in the verbal sparring. What was most noticeable about the boy were his penetrating brown eyes. With a look, it seemed, he could take in all that was there to see. He could look into another person's eyes and seemingly look into the very depths of that person's soul.

Joseph's own eyes lit up with the sudden answer to this difficult problem and, to be honest, he thought, this distraction that presented itself in the form of the troubled rabbi. The man's continued presence was keeping him from finishing the table for old Joshua. Joseph knew that the chest could wait a few days but at the same time he did not want to frustrate the distraught rabbi, thereby keeping him in the shop any longer than need be.

Joseph looked at Rabbi Moshe and smiled. "Okay Moshe, you talked me into it," said Joseph. "I'll get this shop started right away on it. How many scrolls will the new chest have to hold?"

"Oh, well, ah, let me think," said Moshe, who was temporarily thrown off balance by the shift in the conversation. "Well, we need one big enough to hold the 39 sacred scrolls and then there are between 15 and 20 commentaries. The old chest was filled to overflowing, so I don't know."

"Well, no bother," said Joseph as he led the rabbi to the door. "Someone from the shop will be over in a while to measure. Don't worry about payment. Because it is for the synagogue there will be no charge. The chest should be done inside a week. Good day, Rabbi Moshe. May the peace of God be with you."

Moshe turned around before the carpenter could shut his door. "One more thing, Joseph," said the rabbi who had put his foot in the door to prevent the closure. "I will pay a fair price for the chest. I insist and I will hear no more on the subject. May God continue to prosper you and your family." Moshe turned and was gone before Joseph could say another word.

Joseph turned and walked back into the shop to where Jesus stood leaning against the wall. As he got closer, Joseph noticed the raised eyebrow and shook his head from side to side. "How do you do that?"

"Do what?" asked Jesus, who lowered his right eyebrow and then raised his left one. "Usually I just stand close to the wall and then lean into it."

"Not that," exclaimed the exasperated Joseph. "How do you raise one eyebrow with out raising the other? "Oh that," said Jesus as he again switched eyebrows. "It's easy, you just do it."

Joseph just shook his head and stared at the boy. He was proud of his oldest son and was pleased with the progress the boy was making as an apprentice carpenter. "Jesus", Joseph said, "How would you feel about taking on your own job? I'm too busy with the table and a half dozen other projects to start on anything new in the next two weeks.

"Does this have to do with the rabbi?" asked Jesus. "What was that all about anyway?"

"The chest that holds the Scripture scrolls broke into pieces the other day and now Moshe won't sleep right until a new one is built," said Joseph. "Do you think you can handle a project like this?" Without waiting for his son's reply, Joseph went on. "You know that the work you do will have to be of the best quality and of the best workmanship. Long after you are gone, the chest, if made properly, will still hold the precious Words of God Himself."

Jesus jumped back from the wall he was leaning on and walked toward his Joseph. While he had worked on many projects with his father over the years, he had never been given a paying job that would be his to start, work and finish. Looking Joseph in the eye, Jesus replied, "I'll build the finest chest that ever sat in a synagogue. I think it only right that the Scriptures should have the best dwelling place when not being used. Yes, father, I can handle this job."

Joseph smiled at the boy's enthusiasm. "Where do you plan to start?" asked the senior carpenter.

"Well you told Rabbi Moshe that someone would be over to take measurements," said Jesus. "I will go over there now, if that's alright?"

"That's fine," said Joseph. "Just make sure you get back here this afternoon. I will need your help to deliver this table — if I can ever get it done.

"What should I tell the rabbi as far as what to charge?" asked Jesus, who fully expected his father to set the price. "I overheard what the teacher said as he walked out the door."

"I don't know," said Joseph, who then went on to instruct his junior apprentice in proper business dealings. "I never quote a price sight unseen. That can get you into a world of trouble and end up losing you a pile of money."

"I see what you mean," said Jesus as his mind raced on the problem at hand. "What I'll do is go over there and see how big the chest really needs to be and then look at the old one. I'll know more after I do the initial measuring."

"That's what I would do," grinned Joseph who was pleased the boy had worked through the problem. "Just remember, this is your job to do from start to finish. I'll look in from time to time but it's yours to work. Whatever price you set, that's what we'll charge."

"OK, it's a deal," said Jesus nodding his head but not really paying attention. The apprentice carpenter's eyes glazed over lost in thought. Joseph smiled inwardly at the fact that he would not have to deal with Moshe; he would simply refer the rabbi to his son. Jesus skipped out of the shop and headed across town to the synagogue, showing the excitement that only comes with doing something that he had always wanted to do for the first time. He stopped only briefly to take the special rods that his father always kept by the door so he could measure and plan.

"Remember, be back this afternoon," yelled Joseph at the retreating back of Jesus.

Three

Mothers of Pride and Grief

It had been a difficult morning for Mary. She bent down to retrieve the shards that were all that was left of the water pot that had just fallen from the head of her oldest daughter, displaying the patience that she knew only God could give to a mother. While just 8-years-old, Miriam was expected to go with her mother every morning to the small creek that ran alongside the town of Nazareth and bring water back to the house for the family to use that day.

Miriam was naturally clumsy. The evidence of that was the half-dozen or more pots that lay in ruin from her handling or rather mishandling that were strewn along the path from the family's house to the running water. "I'm sorry mama," Miriam said as the tears poured from her eyes. "I just can't get the balance right and it's too heavy, it hurts"

Mary looked at the girl with compassion. "Miriam, this is one of the main duties of a good wife. In just a few short years some man may ask your father for your hand," said Mary who had said these very words many times before. This is something that you will have to do for the rest of your life. Only in the palace of Herod is there a well with flowing water."

"I know, I know," sniffled the little girl. "But it's too heavy for my small head."

"Miriam, get up," replied Mary, whose allotment of patience dried up like the dropped water on the ground. "Your pitcher was only half full. When I was your age and size, I hauled full pitchers of water. Come on, I don't know what I will tell your father." The mother and daughter were still discussing the techniques of water pot balancing just inside the town's gates when Jesus approached them on his way to the synagogue. As Mary paid half attention to her downcast little girl, she watched as her oldest son approached. Soon he would be a man, she thought. As he came running up she noticed that he was excited about something, a fact that she could plainly see by the look on his face and the skip in his step.

As Jesus stopped to say hello and good morning to his mother and sister, he found that he was out of breath. He had been in a hurry to get to the synagogue to start the survey of the Torah shelve and having to lug the measuring poles was something that he wasn't used to.

"Good morning mother," said Jesus, taking a big breath. Then looking down at his sister, he noticed that her eyes were puffy, like she had been crying. "What's wrong, Miriam?" In response to the question, Miriam started to breathe deep and her eyes watered up like she would start crying again.

Seeing this Mary stepped in and said, "She tripped and broke another water pot, and she's afraid that your father will lose patience with her when he finds out and will give her the correction she deserves."

Jesus looked at his little sister and asked his favorite rhetorical question, "What am I going to do with you, girl?" Miriam smiled at him sheepishly, hoping that he could make things right.

"Why don't we practice balancing the pot tonight after supper?" said Jesus. "If father gives you any grief, I'll offer to pay for the pot," said the older brother knowing full well that his father Joseph would never think about taking money for an accident from one of his children. Even, Jesus thought, from Miriam, who was an accident waiting to happen. Miriam gave Jesus a hug and ran off toward the center of town and to the house that Joseph's family called home. Mary watched as she ran off and smiled, pleased that her little girl could have such a wonderful brother to dry her tears.

"So, what has gotten you so excited?" Mary asked. She noticed that the boy had grown just as tall as she was and that when they talked they looked one another right in the eye.

"Father has given me a real paying job to work on without him," answered Jesus. "I'm on my way to the synagogue with these measuring rods right now to start working on a new Torah chest. My first job will be to build the Lord God a place for His Word, when it is not in use."

Mary looked into the eyes of Jesus for a long moment. In that moment she remembered what some of the people had said before her eldest son was born and wondered that it was any accident that this would be Jesus' first job. She would have to have a long talk with him soon ... but not today.

"That's wonderful son, make sure you do a good job. Now get going, you're being paid to work and build, not pass the day with your mother," said Mary, with a laugh in her voice.

"Bye, mother," said Jesus, who then sprinted off toward the other side of town. "Peace be upon you."

As Jesus ran off, Naomi came walking up from the creek, balancing her water pot with the grace, strength, and poise that came from having done the task since she was Miriam's age. "That boy of yours has certainly grown," she said, stopping beside Mary. "It seems like just yesterday when you and Joseph and Jesus moved back into the town. The boy was grown only up past my knees and would barely speak a word and when he did, it was in Aramaic. Not even proper Hebrew."

"Yes, he is getting big," laughed Mary, as she picked up her own water pot and balancing it on her head fell in step with the other woman as they continued into the town. "He can still speak Aramaic, too. He learned it as a crib language while we were in Egypt," boasted Mary, who knew that only the best-educated men would ever speak two languages fluently.

"I spoke with your husband this morning about fixing my door. He said he would be over this afternoon to look at it," said Naomi, who then stopped and took the pot from her head. "Oh, Mary, what am I going to do with my son? Only 17 years of age and already Simon comes home drunk every night," said Naomi. "How come he can't be like your Jesus? Obviously, your boy is already working and helping his father. Oh, I wish that Jarus had not died in the field last year. My boy needs his father."

Mary, not really knowing what to say to the distraught mother, just listened in sympathy before offering her friend what she could. "Would you like me to have Joseph talk to the lad while he is over fixing the door?" asked Mary.

Naomi nodded in relief. "Thank you, yes," said the still grieving widow. "I don't want to have to take the situation to the elders if I don't have to." As a widow it was her right to take her son before the town elders, but she knew that her son was hurting as much as she was from the loss of Jarus. She also knew that the elders could be harsh and if she could, she wanted to spare him any more pain.

Four

Counting the Cost

Jesus arrived at the synagogue and immediately went to work. "What a mess," he said out loud, mostly to himself. He noticed the Torah scrolls stacked in a corner and vowed that they would not be there very much longer. He measured the old Torah chest with the rods that he had brought from his father's shop. He observed how old the wood of the decimated chest was and saw that the pieces of the broken boards were dry because its builder had not used any preservatives or coatings to ensure the durability of the wood. Jesus promised himself that the chest he would build would be around long after he was dead and gone.

Jesus brought the scrolls out into the middle of the floor, off the dais where the rabbi presided and down where the students sat. He lined up row after row of the scrolls, side by side, until he had a good idea of how big to make the chest. It was apparent that the old chest was not made to contain and hold that many scrolls and was just one more reason why Jesus was now called upon to build a new one.

After doing some calculations in the dirt of the floor, Jesus figured that a chest 1 1/2 cubits tall, 2 1/2 cubits deep and 4 cubits long could contain all the scrolls laid out, plus have room for future additions to the synagogue's library. Jesus got up to go after he finished the measuring. He painstakingly moved the Torah scrolls back into the corner where he had taken them from, even going so far as to put them back in the order in which he had found them. Then he folded up the rods, after marking on them the measurements for the chest that he would build and made for the exit.

As he went to leave, he looked around the small town synagogue and wondered about his future. He would be coming here with the other boys his age soon. It was here that his formal education would begin, even though his father and mother had been teaching him at home. He had always attended services on the Sabbath with his family, but he had to sit in the balcony with the women. Soon he would be able to sit on the ground floor with the men. Jesus smiled. He knew he would be at the head of his class, even ahead of the older boys, once he started attending. While the other boys attended out of duty and obligation, Jesus loved the Torah. He loved listening to the old stories of the prophets and the patriarchs.

He had recited from memory out of the family Torah scroll of Isaiah, one evening, word for word for what seemed like an hour, a feat that had amazed his parents. The recitation had been the family's devotional reading the previous night and it seemed, Jesus explained to his dumbfounded parents, that he had memorized every word.

Jesus turned to go with a sigh. He felt that there was so much to learn and so little time. He knew he was still young, yet he felt at the age of 11 to be running out of time.

Five

Table Service

Jesus returned back to his father's shop just in time to help deliver old Joshua's table. The table was over 10 feet long and made out of solid oak. Joseph himself had obtained the wood from the Hebron area, south of Jerusalem. Father and son loaded the three sections of the table onto the back of a cart that Joseph used just for deliveries of large pieces or the hauling of raw materials.

As they were leaving, Mary came out of the family's dwellings that were above the workshop on the second floor. "Joseph, are you going to Naomi's after you and Jesus get done delivering the table?" she asked.

"Yes, that was my plan," said Joseph. "I'll probably send Jesus back with the cart while I go have a look at that door."

"Could you have a talk with Simon?" asked Mary. "Did she tell you how the door was broken? Naomi is worried that something is really wrong with him." Mary looked at her husband to see if he would agree to the task. Joseph was a man who normally didn't involve himself in other people's business and was often reminding her to do the same. Joseph returned his wife's gaze while he thought through how much he wanted to get involved in what was clearly a private family matter. He made his decision with the thought that if he were dead and gone, he would want one of the men of the town to have a talk with a child of his that was going astray.

"OK, I will talk to the boy," Joseph said nodding his head. "If not this afternoon, then tonight at the council fire."

"Thank you," said Mary who stood on the tips of her toes and gave her husband a kiss. She turned and went back up the stairs to their house. She was just starting to prepare the evening meal for her family and the hungry workingman who provided the food that they would eat. Before she went through the door, she turned back at the threshold to glance at her husband and son as they transported the table down the narrow street. From the looks of it, she thought, there were now two of them.

The trip to go across town to the rich man's house took the master and apprentice carpenters 20 minutes. Joshua was one of the wealthiest citizens in the small town that was built on a hill overlooking the rich plains of lower Galilee. He was a tailor who provided clothes and cloaks for not only Nazareth but also for the closest town five miles to the southeast, Japha, and the biggest city in the region to the north, Sepphoris, only eight miles away. Because of the Jewish law of loaning money against a person's cloak, Joshua was also the town's banker and moneylender. While he could not charge his fellow Jews interest, according to the Law of Moses, he had no quibbles about charging the Greeks, Romans, and even the hated Samaritans the going rate, which, lately, was at 13 percent but had been as high as 21 percent in the recent past.

Joshua clearly had the biggest house in the small town. Joshua had built, at about the time Joseph and Mary had moved to the town 10 years before, a three-story mansion, made of hand-made bricks, oak, and marble. It was unlike the two-story mud-brick houses that most of the people lived in. The tailor's residence had an open courtyard in the middle of the four-sided building and the interior walls were all finished with whitewash or expensive wood paneling. A person could look down from the four roof patios that faced the four corners of the earth on a clear night and see the lights of neighboring communities far in the distance.

Joshua was waiting at the gates of his home for the two carpenters as they rolled the cart up. "Welcome to my home, Joseph bar Jacob and Jesus bar Joseph," said Joshua formally. "May the peace of God be with you both while you are in my house."

"Peace be unto you and your household, Joshua bar Er," said Joseph, who fell comfortably into the ritual greetings that were part of his culture. "I have the table as you can see. Where can we put it for you?"

"I have a room specially prepared for it upstairs," said Joshua, smiling from ear to ear. "Do you need me to help you?"

"That is not necessary, my friend," said Jesus who then gestured at Jesus. "I brought my strong son here. Between the two of us, we won't have any problems."

Joshua's table was deposited at the far end of the dinning room. The master and apprentice carpenters had to make three separate trips to the upper room on the south side of the third floor.

"Here is the agreed upon price," said Joshua as he paid Joseph the full amount. "As always, you have completed the job on time."

"I had a horrible time this morning with interruptions," said Joseph. "I even gave Jesus, here his first job to do all by himself.

"Then the Lord God has truly blessed you," smiled Joshua, who then turned to the young man who up until that time had not said a word, but who was grinning from ear to ear. "What will be this first project for you, young Jesus?"

"I will be making a new Torah chest for the synagogue," said Jesus. "I was just over there this morning planning before we came here."

"Well, if you have any of your father's skill, the chest will be most magnificent," said the town's tailor, who then ran his hand over the finished surface of the new table. "I know for a fact that there is more than one board that comprises the top of this table. But to look at it, I can't tell where one piece stops and another begins." Looking at Joseph and then at Jesus, the tailor went on. "I use only your father for any wood work that I have need of. He is the finest wood craftsman in all of Galilee, maybe in all of Israel."

"OK, my friend," said an embarrassed Joseph, who felt suddenly uncomfortable with the praise of his obviously pleased customer. "I am pleased that you are satisfied with the table."

"I know," the tailor said suddenly. "Let us have a drink to celebrate this successful business transaction."

"How about tonight?" suggested Joseph. "Say after the fire?"

"Do you have to go?" asked Joshua. "Surely you can stay for a little while longer?"

Joseph was tempted to stay and fellowship with the elder man. He knew that things had not been good for him in his family life in the past year. The younger of his two sons had left after all but demanding his share of inheritance of his father's money. Now there was little joy left for him as he constantly worried for his son.

The youth had claimed that the little town of Nazareth was too small for the dreams he had for his life and he was tired of living in the boring agricultural crossroads. The young man left on his 20th birthday and the father had not seen nor heard from him since that day. Joseph knew that while Joshua could be tough on his children, as any good parent was instructed to be by the Torah, the carpenter also knew that the tailor loved his children more than life itself. It was only because of this soft spot for his boys that he had parted with money that would have normally been distributed at his death. Thinking of Joshua's son reminded Joseph that he had an appointment with Naomi and her son that afternoon.

"Tonight, Joshua, we will toast the new table. I have another job I promised to attend to," said Joseph, who really did not want to talk with Naomi's son with the smell of wine on his breath.

"Well then, tonight it will be," said Joshua, who then bowed to first Joseph and then, surprisingly to Jesus as well. "May God go with you and keep you until we meet again."

"May God richly bless your house and all who break bread with you at this table," replied Joseph. "Goodbye, my friend. I'll see you tonight." Jesus and then Joseph left the house and made their way to the wagon that was parked out front. "So you want me to take the cart back home?" asked Jesus to Joseph, remembering the conversation between his parents earlier.

"Yes, I need to go survey another job," said Joseph.

"Can I start on the Torah chest when I get back?" asked Jesus, who really wanted to get started on this first project.

Joseph smiled at the enthusiasm of the young boy as he looked at Jesus. "Feel free to use any of the tools you think you might need," said Joseph. "Just make sure to put them back in their place when you're done with them. And make sure you put the cart back in its place also. I don't want to find it just dropped off in front of the shop.

"Do you want me to feed the donkey when I put it back in its stall?" asked Jesus as he grabbed hold of the rope that was tied around the animal's head.

"No," answered Joseph. "I'll feed it along with the others when I get back later this afternoon."

"See you later then," said Jesus as he led the donkey drawn cart back in the direction it had come from. "I'm already hungry. I hope mother is fixing something good for supper."

"She always does," said Joseph. "I'll see you back at the shop." As Jesus went away, Joseph took another street and headed toward the center part of the town. Joseph immediately set about inspecting the broken door when he arrived at the home of Naomi and Simon. Joseph noticed at once that the damage to the door and its jam was fixable. The top hinge was loose. This would require Joseph to reattach the hinge at a different spot on the door. The molding that held the door tight when it was closed was splintered and pieces of it were lying on the ground around the threshold. Joseph fixed the door so that it would stay closed through the night.

"I will need to get some tools and some materials," said Joseph to Naomi, who stood watching the carpenter work. "I have made it so it will be closed throughout the night and I will return in the morning to fix it permanently."

Joseph looked up over the left shoulder of Naomi when he saw Simon enter the front room. The young man's eyes looked bloodshot, and Joseph could tell that he had not been out into the family's field to work that day. Joseph nodded to Simon. "Hello, Simon," said Joseph as a greeting and as a way to strike up a conversation with the sullen and quiet farmer. "Will you be at the fire tonight?"

"Hello, Joseph, peace be with you in this house," said the boy who at the last minute remembered his manners. "Yes, I'll be there."

"May I have a word with you after council is finished?" Joseph asked.

Simon looked over at his mother, as if annoyed with her and suspicious that she may have put Joseph up to the talk. He then looked back at Joseph and said "Sure. It will be no problem if council doesn't take too long. I have things to do tonight and an appointment to keep."

"Good, then I will see you tonight," said Joseph. "May the Lord God bless this home and make it prosper and be at peace." Joseph left the house and headed for home. In the background of the house he had just left he heard mother and son arguing.

As he walked along the streets, Joseph exhaled a sigh of contentment. He was happy that he had gotten much done that day. He was, however, anxious to see his children and wife. It was always a comfort to him to come home to those he loved and to those, he knew, who loved him.

Six

Lost and Found

Joshua went back into his home almost as soon as the carpenter and his son had left. After making a full circuit around his spacious house, he found his wife, Anna, preparing the evening meal in the courtyard. Anna had been the most beautiful woman he had ever laid eyes on when they were first married, but now she looked careworn and tired. Her eyes had the deep lines under them that only many years spent rearing, tending, and toiling with children could produce.

"Whatever it is that you are cooking smells great," whispered Joshua in his wife's ear as he hugged her from behind. "I bet it will taste even better if it's served on our new dining table."

"Did Joseph finish it?" asked Anna, whose eyes lit up and the lines under them seemed to disappear. "Is it up in the room now?" she asked as she turned around to face her husband.

"Yes," said Joshua, who was glad to see his wife smile after so many tears in the last year. "Joseph and his son Jesus have just left after delivering it."

"So that was what all the talking I heard a little while ago was all about," the tailor's wife said. "Why you didn't invite them and Mary to come for supper?"

"I tried to have them stay for a glass of wine," said Joshua. "But Joseph had to go to another job. He said that he would be able to salute with me tonight at the fire."

"Well, we will have a grand dinner upstairs ourselves tonight," she informed him. "I will even set an extra place setting, like we do at Passover. Perhaps the Lord will send Elijah or some other special personage to help celebrate." She busily returned to her chore, humming a Psalm melody and seeming to stand a little taller.

Joshua climbed the courtyard stairs to the north roof, as had been his custom every night for the past year. A friend gave the last report of his lost son to him after traveling the north-south route that passed through Nazareth. Joshua believed that his son had gone north looking for something that didn't exist. Happiness was always to be found with family and friends. Living with strangers could never replace that. While Joshua gazed to the north, he said a quiet prayer. "Oh Lord, protect my son and bring him back to his mother. Oh Lord, please, bring him back to me. Please don't let anything happen to him or punish him too hard for sinning against You."

When Joshua lifted his head to gaze once more before going below to eat his meal, he saw the form of a person, far off, walking slow on the road. The man's head, for a woman would not be alone on the road at that hour before darkness, was bowed low and except for a dirty tunic, he wore nothing else.

Joshua's heart raced as he realized his prayers had been answered. "Thank you, Lord God of my fathers," shouted the man as he raced down the steps two and three at a time, faster than he had descended a flight of stairs since he was a young man. Once he was on the bottom level, Joshua stopped to grab a new cloak that he had just made and to call for his wife.

"Anna, hurry," cried Joshua. "Our son is coming up the road. Without stopping, he motioned to a couple of servants who had been working in the gardens in front of the house to follow along also. He ran until he thought his lungs would burst and only then did he slow down and hurriedly walk the rest of the way.

The ragged traveler had stopped at the sight of the old man racing toward him. With his head bowed he waited for the rebuke that he knew was coming. He didn't know what else to expect, and he prepared himself for the worst. He was hungry, all but naked, and extremely tired. He had not eaten in two days, since he had been thrown some bread by a passing Levite as the holy man traveled the road. He gathered himself to face his father and beg for some food and possibly a place in the stables where he could sleep, if only for the night. He planned to ask his father that he be taken back as a servant instead of a son, if the old man would have him back at all. He knew that his father's servants lived a better life than what he had lived in the past eight months.

Joshua slowed as he approached his son and saw to his dismay that the bones of his second son were showing through his stretched skin revealed by his bare legs and arms that were uncovered to the elements. He saw how his once proud and arrogant son now bent his head and began to fall to his knees. Joshua rushed to his son and gathered him in his arms, not wanting him on his knees. "Oh, my son," cried the old man, who was literally crying. "I thought you were dead and only prayed for a miracle. Oh, thank you, Lord."

"Father, I am so sorry," mumbled the downtrodden man. "I know that I don't deserve ..." The prodigal son, whose name was Samson, started to explain his intentions in a well practiced speech of how his father should take him back.

"There will be time enough, son, to hear your story," said Joshua. "Here put this cloak on, you must be cold." Joshua put the cloak around the shoulders of his wayward son. The garment had been made with the finest linen for the tailor's own private use.

When Samson felt the warmth of the cloak being put around his shoulders he began to cry. "Oh father, forgive me," whispered the broken son. "I have done you so much wrong." This homecoming was more that he had ever counted on or indeed dared to hope for. He was humbled that his father would treat him with so much love after all the wrong he had done to him. He was equally surprised when his father took his right hand in his own.

Joshua knew that his son felt strange and out of place and that he also felt the need for explanations. He would listen to those later. Now he needed his son to feel that he had come home, that he was still a son no matter what he had done and no matter where he had gone. Joshua lifted up the right hand of his son and placed his own family signet ring on his hand using a deliberation that his son could not fail to notice or perceive. Joshua knew that his son would realize that only fellow family members could ever wear the family signet and he also wanted his son to know that, without explanation, he had forgiven him.

Anna reached the reunion and joined in at the moment that the ring had been firmly placed on the finger of Samson. "Samson, Samson, you are home," she cried and then wailed in tears of joy as she hugged her baby boy to herself. "Please forgive me," she bubbled as the hot tears flowed from her eyes. "If I did anything to drive you away, please forgive me."

"Oh, mama," Samson said as a heavy weight lifted from his chest. "I am to blame."

"Come," she said as she turned her boy toward the house. "There is an extra setting at the table tonight to celebrate a new dining table your father had commissioned. This will be a meal that will be twice blessed because you have come home."

"Mother and father, I am not worthy to eat with you," said the dirty man who had been on the road for days. "I would be grateful for anything left over from the servant's meal."

"No son of mine will eat with the servants," said Joshua.

"What is wrong with you, Samson," chided Anna. "You are family and will always be welcome in this house. Come. You are too thin." With a shout of rejoicing and of thanksgiving to the God they served, the three made their way back to the house and ascended the stairs to share a meal with the rest of the household.

Seven

Family Life

Jesus and Joseph reclined at the dining table talking woods and designs for the new Torah chest that Jesus was determined to start building the next day. The meal was lentil soup with fresh made bread, all washed down with a local wine made from the grapes of a vineyard owned by their next door neighbor, Jonathan bar Nun. The small children drank milk produced from the five goats that the family owned for the purpose of beverages and cheese.

Joseph sat in the place of honor, in the middle of the table, as was the custom of a father in his own house. Jesus sat at his right hand, as was the tradition of the oldest son. To Jesus' right sat his brothers James and Jude. James was 10 years old and Jude was five years old. Neither of the younger sibling brothers seemed interested in the conversation going on between their older brother and father.

Jude was playing with the a crust of bread, seeing how much soup he could sop up with a piece of bread before the crust, with a splash, would break off into pieces and drop into the clay bowl in front of him. James was playing a game of stare-out with Miriam, who was sitting to the left of Joseph.

"You blinked," cried Miriam to James as the latter was distracted by a piece of Jude's experimental bread plopping into the bowl.

"That doesn't count," said James indignantly. "I was distracted by Jude. You don't even know the rules of this game anyway. You're just a girl."

"Girl or not, I know enough about a game of stare to know that the first one to blink loses," Miriam said, not backing down to her pain of a brother. "The whole point is not to become distracted by anything."

"You just know girl rules," said James whose voice was steadily rising as he tried to intimidate his sister. "I could never lose to you anyway."

"Well, that is just what you did," yelled Miriam who was not about to be over talked by her obnoxious brother.

"Both of you be quiet," said Mary who had just about had enough of the two squabbling siblings. "Quit your fooling around and both of you eat your suppers." Both just stared at each other and, with an unheard challenge, the game started afresh. To the left of Miriam were her two younger sisters, Lydia and Rachel. The girls were twins and, at the age of six, kept their mother busy. Across from James and Jude were another set of twins, Joses and Simon. The babies were just in that stage where they were learning to eat at the family table but needed their mother close by to avoid a mess that could mount faster than snow in a blizzard if left unattended.

The family was deemed blessed by most of their neighbors. Mary had not lost any children in childbirth and had given birth to two sets of twins. Those who knew him regarded Joseph as an honest and hard-working man.

"If you want to make a proper Torah chest, it needs to be made out of acacia and it needs to be the same size as the Ark of the Covenant was. After all, in a way, the chest serves the same purpose as the ark, if you think about it," said Joseph.

"How will I find the specifications for the ark?" asked Jesus.

"In the Torah," answered Joseph. "God showed Moses how to make it and with what kinds of material to use. In the morning, go back to the synagogue and ask Moshe for the scroll that describes this. When you have the measurements, come back to the shop and we will see if we have the materials for it or if a short trip to the coast is needed." The meal ended with Joseph rising first.

"I must go to the fire," Joseph stated to his family. "I promised Joshua that I would have a cup of wine with him in celebration of the table I made for him. He has given me much business through the years and I would not want to offend him by being rude." With that Joseph went into the other room to fetch his cloak and yarmulke and then exited down the side stairs. He could see the fire already started at the gates of Nazareth and knew that the council would be starting shortly.

Eight

A Feast is Declared

The group of about seventy-five men stood as they watched Joshua approach the fire. The town elder could usually be found at the fire every night in fellowship with the men of the town and to judge the legal cases that were occasionally brought before them. Tonight, he approached the fire with a smile on his face and a visitor at his side.

Standing opposite the elders, yet close to the fire, Joseph saw who it was that accompanied the tailor. Malachi, Joshua's oldest son, was on his father's right hand side as usual, walking tall, yet with a disappointed crook to his brow. On Joshua's left strode Samson, looking like death warmed over and walking with his head down.

Joshua asked leave of his fellow elders for the opportunity to address the assembled men of Nazareth after the initial greetings around the fire were completed. The elders immediately granted the request, knowing that their curiosity was about to be assuaged with what the tailor had to say.

"My fellow citizens of Nazareth," started Joshua, who when giving speeches tended to be formal his manner of talking. "Today my son Samson, who I thought to be dead, has returned to me alive." When the tailor said this he motioned at his younger son, who briefly raised his head before lowering it once more. "It would give me great pleasure if all of you and your families would come to my house on the morrow at about this time," continued Joshua. "I am giving a feast of thanksgiving to the Lord of Hosts, God Almighty, who has kept my son safe and alive this past year." The men of the village began to cheer, but then became quiet when Joshua continued talking.

"Please feel free to bring all that are under your roof to the celebration," said Joshua, who had paused in his speech until the men quieted down. "Tomorrow morning, I will kill a fatted calf for the celebration and as a token of the sacrifice that I will give to the Lord when next I am in Jerusalem." The men of the town gave a great shout and as one assured Joshua that they would be present to celebrate his good fortune and abundant blessing.

Joseph was glad for Joshua and was sure that Mary would want to go and be with Anna and the other women the following night. As he sat listening to Joshua finish his story and invitation, his eyes glanced at the face of Malachi, who at the mention of his brother being thought dead and coming back to his father, rolled his eyes, shook his head and looked away from his father. Joseph wondered if maybe the older son was jealous with all the attention being paid to his brother. He felt the need to talk to the young man and see if he could help. After all, the carpenter thought, Joshua had been very good to him and his family. It was the least he could do.

With the thought of helping another young man, Joseph's eyes traveled the crowd until they settled on Simon, who was at the edges of the crowd. His face looked torn between happiness and deep sadness. Standing next to him was Tobias who was looking happy indeed at the prospect of a feast and with free wine flowing for an entire evening. Other business was covered, but in truth, nothing much was happening that week, because of the planting season. The men decided to wait to cleanse and refill the well that had been contaminated and made unclean until the following week, after the crops were put in.

As the evening fire came to a close with the traditional recitations of the Proverbs of Wisdom, said to have come from King Solomon, the men once more pledged to Joshua that they would be in attendance the following night. Joseph for his part immediately got up and took the most direct path to Simon, wanting to catch him before Tobias dragged him off once more.

He was almost too late and had to jog a little bit before he tugged on the sleeve of the young who was heading to the rundown house of Tobias.

"Simon," called Joseph. Simon turned around, and in his eyes Joseph could see that he had just then remembered promising this carpenter a word after the fire.

"Hello, Joseph," Simon said as his eyes fell to the ground.

"I thought maybe you had forgotten that I had asked for a word with you," said Joseph, knowing that the boy had tried to leave before he was cornered. Looking at Tobias, who had stopped to wait for Simon, Joseph said, "I think you can go on ahead, I have business with Simon here and it may take awhile." Tobias turned to leave without a second thought, his mind only on the wine that he would soon be consuming. He thought that if the boy weren't with him, there would be more for him.

Simon watched Tobias leave without a question and wondered why his friend had not spoken up for him. He then felt an arm come across his shoulder and was led back toward the fire.

"I saw the door this afternoon and I saw you," began Joseph. "You sure did a number on it. It will probably cost your mother money that would have been spent better on winter clothing or travel money."

"Well," said Simon. "It was an old door."

"I think you know that drinking too much wine can make you feel better for a little while, but yet make you feel sick the following day," said Joseph, who pretended not to hear the boy's lame excuse. "I think you can figure out what causes the headaches and figure out to go easy on the wine. What I am worrying about is your family's fields." With that, Joseph turned to look Simon in the eye. "Your family depends on the wheat that comes from those fields. Simon, you are the man of the family now," Joseph said as Simon averted his eyes from that of the older man and rested his chin on his chest.

"Hurting and losing yourself in the wine of forgetfulness is also hurting your mother and sisters who look to you for their provision," continued Joseph when Simon said nothing. "Causing needless damage does no one any good and takes hard earned money away from the family." Resting both of his hands on Simon's shoulders and bending his head so that he could continue to look at the young man's eyes even though Simon had bowed his head, Joseph continued his speech.

"Simon, whether you like it or not, you are not your own man. Your mother needs you now that her husband has been taken from her. It was not your father's fault that his heart stopped beating while working in the field. It is certainly not your fault that you have to grow up faster than expected. Fault or no, it is reality and a true man always deals with the realities of life and does not allow his mind to mull over the 'what-might-have-beens.'

Simon was now crying, for he had a tender heart and the very center of his being had been pierced through and through with the words that had been aimed at him. Joseph, for his part, held the young man in place of the father who could never return, and hoped that just a stern talking to would turn him from a path of destruction and futility.

Composing himself after crying his last tear, Simon vigorously shook the hand of Joseph. "I need to be getting home, Joseph," said Simon. "I'll need to be out in the fields early tomorrow. Thank you for your help." Turning, the young man left at a fast gait, going in the opposite direction from Tobias.

Joseph turned to return home to his family when he spotted the waving hand of Joshua on the opposite side of the fire, signaling him to come over. Joshua, still in an exuberate mood, poured Joseph a cup of wine as the carpenter circled the fire and made his way over to the happy elder.

"I remembered as I saw you talking to young Simon over there that you had promised to have a cup of wine to celebrate the table you built for me," said Joshua as he handed the cup to Joseph.

"I trust the table stood still for the food that was served on it tonight?" asked Joseph with a smile.

"Oh yes indeed, what a first meal the table saw, with my whole family gathered around," said Joshua. "I am extremely grateful that you were able to finish it on time. As it turned out, it was just in the nick of time to serve my son his homecoming meal."

"May God richly bless your reunited household," said Joshua as he grasped the forearm of Joshua.

"And may God continue to bless you, Joseph," returned Joshua. "Perhaps you will have another set of twins?"

"I think I have blessings enough in that area, my friend," said Joseph. "Mary and I will come tomorrow night. We will see you then." With that, the men headed toward their respective homes.

Nine

Balancing Lessons

Joseph arrived home that night to an interesting sight. Miriam was balancing a water pot on her head while Jesus and James looked on. Curiosity got the best of Joseph and he slowed up his walk and moved to the side of the road, under the shadow of an olive tree, in order to watch the unfolding drama.

"Come on you can do it," encouraged Jesus as his sister locked her knees after rising with a pot filled one quarter way full with dirt. Except for the glow of the oil lamps coming from the interior of the house, the front courtyard of the combination carpenters workshop and family residence was in darkness. "I can't see to start walking and the pot is hurting my head," whined Miriam as she moved to take a first step.

"What ever you do, don't look down to see where you're going!" exclaimed Jesus, who had visions of pot shards scattered around the front yard and having to explain to his mother and father why another pot had been destroyed.

"But how will I know where to go?" exclaimed Miriam in a huff.

"She will never be able to do it," said James, with the glee and negativity that was reserved for the torture of a little brother or sister. "Come on Jesus, let's go inside and play a game of cliket. I will let you have the white stones if you let me go first."

"I'll go inside in a minute and if we do play, we'll draw lots for who goes first, like always," said Jesus, who desperately wanted to get rid of his little brother. James, it seems, was always putting Miriam down, and his presence here tonight would not help the lessons "Why don't you go upstairs and set up the board," said Jesus. "I'll be up in a few minutes."

"OK, but I think you're wasting your time, brother," said James, not resisting the impulse to cast a last insult. "She's as clumsy as a field ox and as ugly as one too. I think I will just have to tell father about the water pot today. With your luck, Miriam, you'll probably get beaten."

"If you tell, James, I won't play cliket with you tonight," said Jesus, trying to head off a major fight between his younger siblings.

"Please don't tell," cried Miriam, who was slowly coming to the verge of a major fit. "I don't want to get in trouble."

"I'll think about it," said James, with what could only be described as a demonic smile. Laughing at his own cleverness, James went back up the side stairs that let into the living quarters of the village carpenter's home.

"Are you ready now?" asked Jesus of his sister, who, by the look of it, was close to tears.

"Yes, I'm ready, but I'm going to hit James hard when we get done here. I hate him, Jesus. I hate him for what he says to me," said Miriam.

Jesus raced up to Miriam and looked her in the eye. "That was a crueler thing to say about him than anything else he has ever said or done to you," Jesus said. "Don't let those thoughts go to your heart, they are from the evil one and will ruin you."

"Now, turn around and face the city gate," said Jesus. "See the dying embers of the fire?"

"Give me a second; it's hard to turn around with this pot on my head. Ok, yes, I see it, it's right over there," said Miriam, who unknowingly looked right past her father under the tree.

"Walk toward the fire, looking at it and not down at your feet," Jesus instructed, suddenly figuring out the girl's problem. Miriam walked 15 paces with the pot balanced perfectly on her head. The water jar neither swayed nor did the little girl trip and fall.

"I'm doing it, I'm doing it," shrieked Miriam. Stopping in mid-stride, Miriam whirled to tell Jesus how excited she was when the pot fell off her head and headed for the ground.

Jesus saw the pot sliding off Miriam's head and without a moment's thought he raced to his sister's side and just managed to pick the falling jar out of the air at knee level. In the process of rescuing the clay jug, Jesus ended up skinning both knees and the back of his left hand as he fell from being off balance.

Being an emotional and somewhat dramatic young lady, Miriam screamed at the sight of Jesus rolling, clutching the heavy water pot to his chest, and grunting in pain from his injuries. Joseph also heard his son's exclamation of pain and left his hiding place in the shadows to see what had happened. When Miriam had walked with the pot, she had gone out of the light of the oil lamp and Joseph could only listen to what was being said.

Jesus recovered and stood up. "Be quiet, Miriam," he said, rebuking her for being so loud. "You'll bring mom out and then that will be the end of your practice lessons."

"I think the lessons are over for tonight any way," said Joseph, approaching his two children with the pride, fear, and amusement most fathers feel at moments like these. "How are you son? I heard you take a fall."

Jesus put down the water pot and gave himself a once over. "I think I'm all right, I feel some blood on my knees and my hand hurts a little, but I don't think any bones are broken," he answered.

"So what is this all about? I've been watching you two for the last few minutes and I still can't figure out what's going on," asked Joseph.

Jesus jumped in to explain before Miriam could start with a sob story that would include dramatic hand flapping and the obligatory tears.

"Miriam broke another water pot today on her way back from the creek," started Jesus, who then told of the children's plan of practicing that evening. "I figured out what she was doing wrong, dad. She was walking, trying to look down at her feet … you know … to make sure she wouldn't trip on anything and fall. Because of the movement of her head, the pot would slide forward on the top of her scalp, hurting her. Because of her discomfort, she would move her head even more and the pot would fall off."

"All you need to do, Miriam, is to pick out an object far enough out in front of you so that your head will always stay level," explained Jesus as he turned to his little sister. "If you do that, the pot won't fall off your head and it won't hurt either."

"But how do I keep from tripping on a rock?" asked Miriam.

"While you're looking out in the distance, look at the ground you will walk over, Miriam," Jesus explained. With a smile, he added with the laughing sarcasm that only a brother possesses, "after all, that's how everyone else walks."

Joseph looked at Miriam with disbelief in his eyes and frustration tinged with anger in his voice. "You broke another one? How come your mother didn't tell me of this?" exclaimed Joseph. "Miriam, I am a carpenter, not a potter. If you keep this up, I will have to spend all of our money on pots and we will have nothing left over for anything else."

Miriam looked at her father as tears welled up in her eyes. "I'm sorry, dad. I didn't mean to break them."

"Father," Jesus, said, not wanting Miriam to go to pieces for the second time that day. "I don't think she will be breaking anymore pots. If she does, I'll pay for them if you want. I'll pay for the pot today out of the money I earn from making the Torah chest."

Joseph looked at his two children and just shook his head. One had the emotional stability of free flowing honey, while the other, it seemed, was always ready to take on other people's problems.

"Maybe I overstated the money problem a bit," admitted Joseph. "I'll just have to sell one of you children. Any volunteers?" asked the joking father as he ran his rough, calloused hands through his children's hair.

"Come on you two," said Joseph. "It's getting late and you, Jesus, have a lot of work ahead of you tomorrow. Let's go inside and let your mother see to your knees and hands." With that Joseph and his two children went inside. A few minutes later, the loud travails of a Jewish mother tending to an injured child were the only sounds that could be heard in the surrounding neighborhood. With all the commotion, Joseph never did get around to telling his family of Joshua's good fortune in having his son return.

Ten

As Was His Custom

Later that night, after his mother had finished fussing over him and applying the salve that would speed healing to his knees, Jesus made his way to the rooftop patio before going to sleep. As long as he could remember and, of course, as long as he was old enough to be able to climb the stairs, he had been coming to the roof to pray to the Creator of the World. His parents were aware that he spent time every night on the roof before bedtime, but had never asked the purpose of his nightly ritual. To Jesus, as he looked at the sky above him, full of stars and wonder, his nightly visit with his heavenly Father was no ritual, it was life itself.

"Hello Father, how are you tonight?" started Jesus in a conversation that little resembled the "prayers" that were prayed at the synagogue. "I hurt myself tonight, but thank you from keeping me from real harm. Please speed the healing process, especially in my knees; they hurt every time I bend them. Thank you for showing me the hate in Miriam's heart. Show her that to love those who do her wrong is the way to please You. Oh God, please bless my father's business and help my mother with the chore of raising us kids.

Father, please bring Joshua's son back to him. He looked so sad and his heart was so heavy. I could feel his despair and concern. Show me or tell me if I should say or do anything for him, Lord, and I will do it." A tear escaped down Jesus' face as he looked up at the night sky. "Show me your will as I begin to make the Torah chest that will house your Words. I pray that you fill me with all knowledge and wisdom, as you did with the craftsman of old, so that what I build will be found worthy in your sight."

Jesus stopped talking and was silent, becoming very still and not moving his body in any way. To a stranger observing him for the first time, it would seem that he was in a trance or was simple minded, but neither was the case. Jesus had discovered years ago that it was only when he was still and quiet was it possible that he could hear what God had to say to him. He had often wanted to speak with Rabbi Moshe about taking time out to listen for God's answer after prayers at the synagogue, but for some reason, the Father told him that the rabbi would not understand. God had told Jesus that the people were more interested in the ritual of praying than in actually talking with Him. God had told him that was one of the primary reasons that he, Jesus, was there on Earth. Jesus knew that he had several things to do while on the Earth, but he also knew that none of them except for prayer needed to be done for many years to come.

Receiving assurance from his God that the reunion that he prayed for had taken place that very night between Joshua and his son, Jesus thanked the goodness of his Heavenly Father's heart. After 10 minutes of listening for his Heavenly Father's voice and receiving instruction from Him, Jesus said amen and made his way back down to the room that he shared with his brothers and sisters. He noticed that his knees felt better already and he smiled in appreciation for his entire family – for Mary and Joseph, his earthly parents, and for God Almighty, his Heavenly Father, who was just as real to him as all the rest of them.

Eleven

Building the Chest

Wednesday morning began early for Jesus as he awoke with a start. He knew that he had a full day in front of him and he was normally not one to sleep in. As he looked around the room where he and his brothers and sisters slept, he noticed that everybody else was still asleep. When he moved to get up he winced in pain. His knees that had been skinned and bruised the night before had scabbed over during the night and now were sore and tender. He rolled over on his left side and put his left hand down on the ground to help propel him to his feet he nearly screamed out in pain as the hand collapsed from his own weight.

Holding the hand up to his face he was reminded of old Moshe the rabbi and his disfigured right hand. Thanking his heavenly father for injuries that would heal and that nothing that he did last night would be permanent, he rolled to his right. Slowly he drew his knees up to his chest and bent them as far as they would go yet not so far as to break open the scabs. Then he pushed off with his good right hand from the floor of the second story room and vaulted to his feet with the agility that only someone under the age of 15 possesses.

He hurried to the door that would take him downstairs to the shop after putting on his tunic. He was surprised to see that it was still dark outside as he made his way to the family privacy hole that was in the northwestern corner of the family grounds.

After relieving himself, Jesus made his way back to the shop were he washed his hands and studied the poles that he had used to measure the old chest. The thought of food didn't even enter his mind and he instinctively knew that his mother would call for him when the morning meal was ready.

Joseph came down to the shop 15 minutes after Jesus had started working and was at first surprised to see the boy. Usually he was alone at this time of the morning and could get many tasks done without distractions.

"You're up early," said the master carpenter over a yawn. "Starting on the chest?"

"Yep," said Jesus without looking up. "I wanted to see what kinds of wood we have here before I go over to the synagogue."

"Well, don't go over too early," cautioned Joseph. "Rabbi Moshe sleeps late whenever he doesn't have school to teach." He left Jesus engrossed with his project while he went out the back entrance of the shop to feed the sheep and milk the goats that were penned at the rear of the building.

After this normal six-day-a-week chore, Joseph brought the milk upstairs to his wife who was busy making breakfast for her large family. Five minutes after the delivery of the milk, the morning meal was served.

"Jesus, breakfast is ready," called Joseph from the top of the stairs.

"I'm not hungry right now," Jesus said as he continued to work. "I'll grab something later."

"You can come up and eat now or wait until another meal is served," Joseph said with an edge to his voice. "Your mother is not running a tavern up here."

"I'll be up in a minute," Jesus replied with surrender in his voice. "It was worth a try," he said out loud to no one in particular.

After a quick meal of cheese, bread, and goat's milk, the family broke up to attend to the tasks at hand. Grabbing James by the hand, Joseph headed off to the family fields, leading an ox, to start sowing the season's crop of wheat.

Jesus, who normally accompanied his father in the field, stayed behind to work on the chest. His father would be back at noonday to eat and work in the shop while the sun was overhead and at its hottest.

Jesus headed over to the synagogue after drawing what he thought the chest would look like on a special slate stone that his father kept for just that purpose. He was hoping to talk to the rabbi and to find out from him what the dimensions of the Ark of the Covenant were.

He entered the synagogue just as Moshe was leaving after his morning prayers. He asked the rabbi if he would like a chest in the exact dimensions of the Ark.

"I don't know. The Law says that no one should make anything that belonged in the Temple for personal use," said Moshe.

"Wasn't the Ark covered in pure gold?" asked Jesus.

"Why yes it was, Jesus," answered the surprised rabbi. "How did you know that?"

"I think you read that particular passage in the Law a few years ago," said Jesus. "This chest wouldn't be overlaid in gold so it wouldn't be an exact replica.

"What made you remember that particular lesson?" asked the astonished rabbi, who assumed that no one listened too closely to any of his lessons.

"I remember all of your lessons, rabbi," answered Jesus without thinking of the extraordinary statement he was making. "I like to listen to the reading every Sabbath."

Shaking his head in disbelief that anyone paid that much attention to what he had to say, Moshe started to speak to change the subject to ease his discomfort that he felt in the presence of this young man before him. "So, about the chest," started Moshe. "I think that … "

"By the way, Rabbi Moshe, I was wondering, why don't we have a quiet time after prayer on the Sabbath?" asked Jesus, who had started speaking at the same time the rabbi did.

"Maybe God would speak to us if we allotted some time for Him to answer?" Jesus said, with a curious look on his face. God had told him that he would not understand, but asking the question this way might give the rabbi something to think about.

Wrinkling his forehead, trying to understand what this carpenter's son was trying to say to him, Moshe did change the subject. "So what did you want again?" asked the rabbi.

"I asked you if you wanted the chest made to the specifications of the Ark?" repeated Jesus, looking at the rabbi with his piercing brown eyes.

"Well, I don't know if that will hold all the scrolls, let me look up the measurements," said Moshe, turning from the boy and going to the corner where the scrolls were being kept.

"Here it is, right after the story of the Exodus from Egypt," said Moshe, after a few minutes of looking. It says here the chests length is to be 2 1/2 cubits; and its height 1 1/2 cubit; and its width 1 1/2 cubit, and also that Bazelel, the master builder, made it out of acacia wood," read Moshe from the scroll of Law.

"If I make it to those specifications, will that be big enough to hold all of these scrolls?" asked Jesus.

"What do you mean, "If I make it?" asked Moshe. "I thought your father would make it."

"He has given the project to me, but don't worry, I will be under his supervision," Jesus said, quickly putting the troubled rabbi's mind at rest.

"Well, I suppose it would hold everything, but it will be tight and there will be no room for more commentaries from new *Rabban* that might come along in the years to come," said Moshe, almost talking to himself and halfway ignoring the young man in his presence.

"Why don't you make it twice the size of the original Ark," said Moshe after a minute or more of consideration. "After all, it will have more to hold than just two tablets, one jar and a walking staff."

"Very well then, I will be on my way," said Jesus. "I was here yesterday to measure and I have the specifications for a larger chest. Jesus turned to the rabbi after he remembered to be professional like his dad had taught him. "If I can get the acacia wood today, the synagogue's Torah chest should be done in about five days. Will that be satisfactory to you sir?"

Smiling at the young man's formal business voice, Moshe told the carpenters apprentice that five days would be fine. "How much do you think it will cost me?" asked Moshe.

Having done the math this morning for the design that he had worked up yesterday, Jesus had an immediate response to the surprise of the rabbi.

"The chest will cost 1 1/2 pieces of silver," said Jesus. "Does that seem a fair price to you?"

After closing his mouth that had fallen open a moment before at this precocious young man who was not yet an adult in the eyes of his religion, Moshe thought over the amount. "Don't you have to ask your father about the amount?" asked Moshe.

"I asked him this morning over breakfast," answered Jesus. "He thought I should charge two full pieces of silver, but left the final price up to me to decide."

Hearing this answer from Jesus, Moshe held out his hand and took the boy's hand firmly. "It's a deal. I will be by in five days for the finished chest," said Moshe.

As he turned to go, Jesus called out from over his shoulder. "My father and I will deliver it, which is our standard business procedure. Have a wonderful day, rabbi, and may the peace of God go with you."

Upon returning home, Jesus ran into his mother and Miriam, also returning from getting the day's water from the creek. Jesus was proud to see Miriam walking tall with the jar on top of her head, not a drop splashing from its full to the brim mouth.

"Look at me Jesus," Miriam called out. "It's even full and I didn't even trip once."

"What did you say to her last night?" Mary asked, clearly astonished at the turnaround in her daughter's performance. "All I heard was Miriam and James arguing and fighting."

"Well, I'm glad I could be of some help," said Jesus, who didn't really want to stand around and talk. "I need to get into the shop and get to work – I only have five days to build the chest. I'll see you both in a couple of hours for the noon meal."

Jesus found that his father had been in the shop since he had been to the synagogue. Lying beside the planning slate where several planks of acacia wood ready to be worked. Studying the plans one last time, Jesus reached down and picked up one of the planks and laid it on the workbench. With that he busied himself with the plans and the wood. The noon hour rolled around and Jesus was lost in his work. He didn't hear his father re-enter the shop until the senior carpenter's hand was placed on his shoulder. Jumping up and emitting a squeak from fright and surprise, Jesus backed away from the hard touch of his father's hand and tripped over backwards onto the planning slate.

"Sorry, son. Didn't you hear me come in? I called down earlier from the family area that the meal was ready," asked a laughing Joseph, who stooped down and gave his son a hand back to his feet.

"I guess I was lost in making this chest," said Jesus, indicating the frame that he had built.

"You have made a good start, come on up for some fruit and a drink," said Joseph. "I came by earlier, after you had left to go to the synagogue. I had to come back to get the yoke harness that I had told James to get. That boy forgets everything, especially if it has to do with work. Anyway, did you talk to Rabbi Moshe?"

"Yeah, he said he wants a bigger chest than what the Ark of the Covenant was," said Jesus. "I quoted him five days and 1 1/2 pieces of silver."

"I still think you should charge him two, but it's your profit margin, not mine," said Joseph, not mentioning that he had supplied the wood and the tools with which the boy was building the chest. As they started climbing the stairs Joseph heard Jesus draw his breath in sharply. "By the way, how are your knees and hand?"

"While I was working I had forgotten all about the pain, right up to the point where you sneaked up on me and scared me," Jesus said, looking down at his father with a strained smile, while still on the stairs. "Then all the pain came rushing back. Thanks a lot, Dad."

After the noon meal, Jesus retreated back to the workshop while Joseph came down for some tools and strips of wood that he would need for Naomi's door. About two hours later, Joseph came back through the shop to drop off his tools. He needed to get back to the field to continue planting and only gave his son's project a cursory once-over.

"It looks like you're doing great," said Joseph. "Can I get anything for you?"

"No," said Jesus. "Everything I need for now is right here."

"Keep up the good work," said Joseph as he walked out the door. "I'll be home before the sun goes down, God willing and James doesn't die."

Several hours later, his father came once more into the shop, dirty from the field, with James in tow. The ten-year-old looked asleep on his feet and was covered from head to toe in the red-brown dirt that was found in the lower Galilee valley. "Remember we have Joshua's party tonight, Jesus," said Joseph with a weary tone to his voice. "Why don't you quit for the night?"

"Is it already that late?" asked Jesus. "I'll be up in a minute; I just need to drive in this last peg into the joint."

"Make sure you clean up before you come upstairs," said Joseph, who had already washed at the bowl that was refilled with water by Mary and Miriam daily. "Your hair is full of sawdust."

Twelve

Party of Thanksgiving

The families made their way through the streets of Nazareth as the sun sank into the western sky, signaling the start of another day. Unlike other cultures, including the Greeks and Roman, Jewish tradition held that a new day started when the sun went down, seemingly singeing the very water of the Great Sea to the west. Thursday of this week would begin with a feast and party for most of the Nazarenes who lived in the small town. The light from the torches that Joshua had set up in his front and central courtyard could be seen from across town, and the aroma of the fatted calf that was cooking made the townspeople's mouths water as they made their way to the feast.

Joseph and Jesus stood waiting for Mary at the edge of the road under the same tree that the father had stood and observed his children the night before. Mary was busy leaving instructions with Lillith, the daughter of the town's blacksmith, who would be looking after the children for the rest of the night. From the sound of it, Mary wanted to make sure that every contingency would be covered. She seldom got to go out with her husband and wanted to make the best of the evening.

"Make sure to put the youngest set of twins to bed soon," yelled Mary as she stood in the doorway. "They will get cranky if you don't. And don't let Miriam and James fight all night either. If you have to, send James to go sleep in the workshop." Mary shut the door and joined her husband and eldest son on the road and started walking toward Joshua's palatial home.

Joshua and his two sons were at the entrance to his front courtyard, greeting guests, when Joseph and his family arrived for the feast. Joseph gave the traditional blessing of peace as they greeted their host for the evening, Mary and Jesus took deep breaths, enjoying the aroma of the cooking veal, while they looked for close friends who had already arrived. In an open pit, the coals of a large cooking fire could be seen glowing as they slowly cooked the young fatted calf. The calf had been cut up into many choice pieces and laid over a metal mesh grate that was propped up by four big, flat rocks. Three of Joshua's servants were tending to the cooking of the meat while hovering in the background, the tailor's wife, Anna, was supervising the pouring of the wine.

"Not this wine, Jerash, this wine needs to age a little while longer. Go get the wine from last year that the master has set aside for himself," Anna instructed. "Joshua has said that only the finest wine and food will be served tonight." The carpenter's family was enjoying a cup of wine while talking with Naomi and her son, who, Joseph noticed, was drinking water. The discussion centered on the freshly planted crops and the rains, both early and late, which would be needed to bring out the heads of grain.

"The fields I've planted in the past couple of days look to be fairly clean," said Joseph. "The weeds should not be a problem this year."

"You are blessed," said Simon. "I was out planting today also and the field looked grown over in nothing but weeds. I will have to give a lot of attention to it when the first shoots of wheat appear." As the last drop of the first cup of wine was swilled into the bellies of the festive guests, a high-pitched bell was rung from the roof of the house, signaling that the feast was about to begin.

Joseph and Mary started moving to the foyer that would take them into the inner courtyard of the house, along with Naomi and Simon. Jesus hung back, not wanting to be caught in the crush of bodies funneling through the breezeway to the inner courtyard. The boy heard without really hearing his father promise Naomi that he would be by in the morning to inspect the door that he had fixed early that day. Normally not one to miss what his father had to say; his attention had been drawn back to the gate.

"I will not go in, father. Take this son of yours and celebrate your heart out," said Malachi. "Maybe I will go out and disappear for a few months, and then you can throw a party in my honor."

"What has gotten into you Malachi," asked Joshua in astonishment of his eldest son's bitterness. "Aren't you happy your brother is home?"

"Father, he took your money – money that he had no right to possess until after you were dead," spat Malachi. "He took that money and broke your heart. He went north to Damascus and squandered your money on strong drink and loose living."

"How do you know all this," asked Joshua. "Samson has not told me anything of what happened to him except to say that when the money ran out, he went to work for a merchant, tending his swine against the dictates of the Torah. Of what he did with the money I gave him, he will not say. He is too ashamed."

"Ashamed? Ashamed?" shouted Malachi, who was so red in the face his father feared the boy would pass out or worse. "Of course he is ashamed. As well he should be. The lion's share of the money you gave him is now in the possession of the most expensive whores in Damascus."

"I didn't know," said Joshua, as he tried to swallow and digest the information he had just received.

Suddenly Malachi ripped his tunic open and hit himself in the chest and began to cry. "How come you have not killed the fatted calf and called the town's people to a party for me? I have done nothing but honor you and mother. I work hard every day to learn the family business and work the fields. Do I have to do something that will shame you before you will honor me?"

Joshua looked at his son in sudden understanding. "My son, you are the beginning of my strength and all that I have, or will come to have, will be yours one day. You will be the master of your brother throughout your lifetime and he will never know independence from you. He has squandered what he would have used to strike out on his own and now, as part of the consequences of his decisions, will always look up to you as master and not as an equal. Your brother knows all of this. He had many hard days on the road coming back to Nazareth to think. He initially had plans to ask that he be a servant and be treated as such. Yet, like you, he is my son. I could not make my son, no matter what he has done, become a common slave in my own house. When he squandered the money on loose living and wild women, he was my son. When he drank the fruit of my labor until he could not see, he was my son. When he ate food that swine had rejected, he was my son. For all that he could do to himself, he could not stop being my son," cried Joshua, as tears streamed down his face to match the ones of his oldest son.

"On the day that I retire and deliver to you the blessing and the birthright that is your heritage to claim, on that day, there will be such a feast as never there was in this town," continued Joshua as his son looked at his father in a different light. "Your brother will never have such a day. For him, this day will be all that he will have. Tonight is not for your brother. The feast in your brother's honor is for me. Don't you understand? My son, who I thought was dead and more than dead, has been given back to me. I am giving this feast to thank the Lord Most High for his protection of someone I love more than myself." Father and son hugged each other, crying in each other's arms. Malachi sobbed for his father's forgiveness for being so self-centered.

"My son, I would be honored if you would come to the place of feast with me and join me as I celebrate the return of my son and your brother."

"For your happiness father, I will. Let us go now while there is still wine to be drunk. The townspeople looked thirsty as they moved to the courtyard," said Malachi with a laugh as he pulled his robe over his tunic to cover the tear he had ripped in it.

Jesus turned away and melted into the shadows against the wall of the house as the two men turned to go into the inner courtyard. As they passed Jesus caught a good-natured question from Joshua to his now reconciled son. "By the way Malachi, I wanted to ask earlier, before you ruined a very expensive one piece tunic. How did you know how Samson had wasted his money? Damascus is over a week's travel by foot and three days by fast horse."

Once again, Malachi's face turned the color of blood as he realized that whatever his father was and no matter how old he had become, he was no fool and was as sharp as ever.

"Father, I need once more to ask forgiveness," began Malachi, with a look of contrition on his face. "I stated earlier that I have never dishonored you but that is not true. My friend Hasim, whose father runs a spice business in the Decapolis, saw Samson about a year ago in Damascus in the circumstances that I described. When he came through town a month after that, he told me all about it. I am sorry, father. I should have told you then where he was. I could have saved you many hours of worry.

"Maybe things have worked out for the best," said Joshua with a slight cock to his head. "Had I known of Samson's condition, I would have went to him and possibly made things worse. Let's just give God the glory for what He has done and say no more about this. Come, let's go. The veal smells delicious."

Jesus followed the hosting father and son into the banquet area that had been set up for the evening in the inner court. The veal was indeed delicious and the wine was the best that Jesus could remember tasting in his short life. After a few more hours of good food, wine, and fellowship, Joseph, Mary, and Jesus made their way back across town to their own more humble home. Their family as well as the rest of the people of the town would need a good night's rest for the labor of the fields that awaited them in the morning.

Thirteen

Finishing Well

Jesus worked steadily on the Torah chest for the rest of the week. He only broke from his labors twice to go out into the field with his father and younger brother and to observe and celebrate the Sabbath. Without the fields and the wheat crop that they produced, Jesus knew that hunger would soon overtake all of them.

He reasoned that it was good for him to know about the different aspects of farming, as he would assume responsibility for the family's fields one day. While he was a carpenter by trade, knowing how to grow one's own food was a prerequisite for everyone who didn't want to go hungry.

After the Sabbath service, Rabbi Moshe had been waiting for him as he descended from the balcony where all the women and males, like himself, who were not yet men of Israel sat while the Torah was read and discussed by the men who sat on the ground floor.

"Hello, Jesus," said Moshe. "How is the chest coming along? Or should I ask your father?"

"The chest is coming along fine," answered Jesus, who was tempted to ask the rabbi if he had given anymore thought to allow a quiet time to listen for God's voice. "The synagogue will not see another Sabbath without it."

"Good," said Moshe with a smile. "Peace be unto you, I need to talk with someone." The rabbi hurried away quickly and was soon into conversation with Joshua.

"Peace be unto you," said Jesus to the back of the retreating rabbi. Jesus left with his family and spent the rest of the day playing games with his brothers and sisters and talking with his parents.

By Sunday evening the chest was completely built. As Joseph inspected the craftsmanship of his oldest son, Jesus stood by, only breathing in big gulps every minute or so.

Finally Joseph stood and looked at his. "I could not have done a better job myself, son. The seams are so matched that even to my trained eye, the sides and lid look like they were crafted out of one big piece."

"I tried to do my best and yet still have it done on time," said Jesus, visibly pleased that his work had passed his father's inspection. "Will you help me deliver it tomorrow?"

"Certainly I will help you," Joseph said with a big grin and then narrowed his eyes. "You still have to collect the fee. For tomorrow, I will be the helper and you will be the master craftsman."

Fourteen

Paid In Full

The cart rolled up to the synagogue with the new Torah chest riding centered on the flat bed and Jesus and Joseph leading the donkey. Moshe came running out of the Synagogue in anticipation of the new piece of furniture and his final atonement in the matter of losing his temper to self-pity. The father and son carpenters lifted the wooden box off the cart and took it into the place of worship. As they made their way down the front raised dais, they could see the Holy scrolls laid out and ready to be placed in the new chest. Sitting the chest down in the accustomed place, beside the rabbi's traditional seat of teaching Jesus turned to Moshe.

"Peace be unto you, Rabbi," said Jesus. "Please come and inspect the chest and see if it is up to your standards and you are satisfied with the craftsmanship."

As Moshe walked again and again around the chest, his eyes grew more distant as if his thoughts were far away. "I'm sure that this chest will make a fine house for the Holy Scriptures," said Moshe, who then turned and faced the carpenters. Holding a small pouch bag in his left hand he reached in and withdrew several silver coins from within. Still with a strange look in his eye, he held out the coins to Joseph. "Payment for a job well done, master carpenter," said Moshe. "This chest is even more beautiful that what I had dreamed."

Joseph made no move to accept the payment proffered him, but cocked his head to one side. "I would accept your praise if I could, Rabbi," exclaimed Joseph. "But, except for providing some materials and inspecting the finished product, I had nothing to do with the construction."

Motioning to Jesus, Joseph went on. "You made the deal with Jesus here and he has built what you ordered. Pay to him both the agreed price and your praise."

Moshe looked at the boy now with clear eyes and a smile broke out upon his face. "I knew with whom I struck the deal," the rabbi said to Joseph with a sideways look. "But the craftsmanship made me think perhaps the boy had a little help." With that Moshe opened up his money pouch yet again and rummaged up another couple of coins. "Perhaps this bonus from a miserly old rabbi will convey to you the depth of my appreciation for your work." Handing over the silver pieces, Jesus realized the rabbi had paid him double the agreed upon price. Seeing the hesitation in his eyes, Moshe said, "Take it, it is more than deserved."

"Thank you, Rabbi Moshe," said the dumbfounded Jesus. Jesus put the silver pieces in a cloth and put the wrapped money in his belt.

"Now that the business part of this deal is over, will you both stay and have a glass of wine to celebrate?" asked Moshe. While usually just a formality that could be graciously declined, especially if early in the morning, the way the rabbi had asked them made them pause.

"It would be our pleasure, Rabbi," said Joseph who motioned for Jesus to follow.

After taking a long drink from his cup, Moshe spoke. "I wanted you to stay and talk with me. I have a proposition to make for the boy here." Jesus was taking a swallow of the wine when the rabbi mentioned him and looked up in curiosity.

"What kind of proposition?" asked Joseph who immediately wondered why the rabbi was taking so much interest in his son.

"The Law states that only a boy of 13 years of age may go to the Temple in Jerusalem to receive his status has a man of Israel," Moshe continued, pretending that he didn't hear the question. "As you know, only a man of Israel may come and take formal instruction at the Synagogue."

Joseph, who knew all of this, shifted his weight impatiently, willing the rabbi to come to his point. What the rabbi said next shocked both him and his son.

"Next month will be Passover and you, Joseph, and I, along with every other man of Israel, will make the journey as required by the Torah to Jerusalem to offer sacrifice and to celebrate the most holy day of our country. I propose that you take Jesus and present him before God and the High Priest. I will write a letter with my recommendation that Jesus be made a man of Israel a year early."

Joseph sat shocked with the idea. While the practice was not unheard of, usually it was held in reserve for sons of leading priests, Pharisees, and other notables who either had the proper connections or who could afford a suitable 'donation.'

"Would the High Priest do that for the son of a small town carpenter?" asked Joseph.

"Your son is an exceptional young man. I think I can assure you that it will happen," said Moshe, who then took another drink and smiled at his two fellow Nazarenes. "The High Priest owes me a favor, you see. A few years back, while he was campaigning for his current post, he assured King

Herod that he would find a rabbi for a small, cross-roads town on the edge of the Galilean/Samarian border." Finishing off the rest of his wine, Moshe stood up and raised his arms as if to display the splendor of his small synagogue. "I told him that one day I would ask a favor of him when I agreed to come up here. I think this may be the best chance I have to collect on that debt."

Fifteen

Worse Than A Thief

As Joseph and Jesus led the donkey and cart away, their mood was more of disbelief than of jubilation. "Can the rabbi really move up my manhood ceremony by one year, Father?" Jesus asked of a thoughtful Joseph.

"It sounds like he thinks he can, and I have heard of such things happening," replied Joseph, who then went on to say what he was thinking out loud. "I've just never heard of it happening to poor Galilean carpenters and farmers before." Father and son continued to discuss the events that had transpired, talking as they walked, and not really paying attention to their surroundings.

Rounding a corner, Joseph looked up to avoid a group of ladies, pitchers of water balanced gracefully on their heads, heading for the cistern well that had been drained because of the dead thief's contamination. At the end of the block of two-storied residences, at the main intersection of the small village, he saw a man sitting at a table, in the very middle of the street.

"Curse the mother who bore you!" Joseph spat with such vehemence, Jesus momentarily stopped walking to look at his father and then looked in the direction that Joseph was looking. The man, a fellow Jew, was well known in Nazareth and was all the more hated for his notoriety. His name was Nathaniel and he passed through town every couple of months, coming and going from his hometown of Caesarea. The man worked for the Roman governor and his purpose in town was always the same. Nathaniel was a tax collector and, except for a swine herder, that was the most odious thing a Jew could become.

"Good day to you, Joseph. Peace be with your house," cried out the obnoxious Nathaniel while Joseph and Jesus were still some 50 yards away. "How is your wife? Is this your oldest son that I've heard so much of? Have you been blessed with any more twins?"

Joseph mentally cringed at the thought of this man having so much private information. It seemed that Nathaniel and every other tax collector knew the most intimate details of even the most private business deals. It was said that they had spies everywhere and had been known to pit father against son and brother against brother by their uninvited presence at major business deals that were supposed to be at secret locations.

"Hello, Nathaniel, I had forgotten that it was time for you to be here again," said Joseph, not bothering to wish peace on what he thought of as trash in human form.

Nathaniel, for his part, acted as if the two of them were long lost friends. "Would you care to have a drink of wine with me?" asked the taxman. "I hear that business has been very good for you and your son. Let's rejoice together."

"Maybe some other time, Nathaniel," said Joseph through clenched teeth. "Let's just get done with the fleecing so I can go my way."

"Now, Joseph," said a smiling Nathaniel, "the roads have to be paid for, and the protection of the legions through the passes of Samaria doesn't come at a cheap price."

"How much?" Joseph said, raising his voice and putting a threatening barb to it that Jesus, who up to now had done nothing but observe what could at best be called constrained hostility, had only heard one time before – when a wild dog had threatened James while working in the fields.

"Well, let's see," said the taxman as he seated himself at the table and, after scrolling through the hated records that he kept, came to what had to be the record on Joseph and his family.

"Since we last met, you have been quite busy. You have had many little odd jobs and quite a few big ones. I met with Joshua earlier and I conducted our business at his new table. That was your handy work; there can be no doubt about that. Good craftsmanship can't be hidden. I have also heard rumors of a new Torah chest being made for the synagogue, was that what you just delivered?"

"How much?" shouted Joseph, feeling shamed at having to endure this traitor of his own people in the middle of the street.

"Five pieces of silver should do the job. Four for Rome and one for my expenses," said Nathaniel, ignoring the raised voice of Joseph as if he wasn't there.

Turning to Jesus, Joseph asked for the money the rabbi had just paid them and putting it together with some of his own threw the money down on the table and walked away.

"Peace be with you, Joseph," said Nathaniel, a little chagrinned that he had been paid so quickly and abruptly. Next time he was in town, he would take a little more time to more accurately find out how much he could tax the carpenter. He remembered a time when half a piece of silver was the going tax for the man.

Sixteen

Good New, Bad News

Joseph didn't talk the whole way home. After unhitching the donkey from the cart, the two entered the shop and prepared to go upstairs for the noon meal. "Jesus, I will repay you the money I used to pay the tax swine," said Joseph, his face now back to his normal golden color instead of the bright red that it had been at the city intersection. "I'm sorry you had to see me lose my temper, but Nathaniel and his sort are worse than the thieving Samaritans. At least they just come out and rob you without having to listen to their insincere banter."

"I was going to give you the money anyway, father. Why does he ask for so much?" asked Jesus, who had not observed this side of the business before today. "How does he know how much to charge? Is there a rate?"

"There is no rate, despite what he says. The tax gatherers take what they think they can get without open rebellion being fomented against them and winding up in a well or with a knife sticking out of them. In truth, I came out well this time. I fear because in my anger I paid him so quickly and flippantly, I will pay a higher price the next time around." As the two climbed the stairs leading to the family living quarters, Joseph suddenly stopped half way up and started breathing heavily.

"What's wrong, Father," asked Jesus with concern.

"Whenever I get upset, I seem to lose my breath, especially coming up these stairs. I'll be all right in a moment," assured Joseph as he took one more breath, while messaging his left arm with his right hand. Finally Joseph started moving up again, seemingly recovered from his breathless episode and Jesus followed along behind him trying not to show his concern.

The midday meal consisted of goat's cheese, dates, and some figs from a tree in the family's fields. Attention was at first paid to the smaller and younger of the kids as they excitedly rehashed their morning adventures. Mary was the one who finally asked how the drop-off of the Torah chest went. Trying and failing to mask his excitement, Jesus rushed into an accounting of the day's events.

"The rabbi really liked the chest, Mom. He thought that Father had made it and even tested the fact before paying me double what the agreed price was," exclaimed Jesus, who by this time was talking faster than a street market vendor. "He also suggested something else, but I think I will let Father tell you."

Joseph looked at his wife and shifted his position at the table to get more comfortable on the pillows that he reclined on. "Rabbi Moshe thinks that Jesus is ready to be confirmed at the Temple now. He wants us to present him to the High Priest for his bar-Mitzvah when it is time to go up to Jerusalem for Passover next month," Joseph said, keeping his attention fixed on his wife and studying her eyes for her reaction.

Not surprising him at all, Mary's reaction and questions were not centered on her son's readiness or abilities. "How much attention will this bring to him? How long will he have to be in Judea? Is it safe?"

Joseph continued to look at his wife as he considered her questions, and seemed to look far away. "I think we will continue this discussion later. I told Jesus I would want to discuss this with you, and while he let me bring it up now, I think I need time to think and pray. I would also like at least one night of sleep between me and any decision I make." Looking a little disappointed, Jesus nodded his head at having the answer put off until at least the next day. Jesus wondered to himself what his parents were protecting him from. Not for the first time, something passed between his parents and, not for the first time, Jesus wondered what it was.

Seeing that at least James and Jesus were done eating, Joseph got up and gathered his two oldest boys to take a trip into the fields. There had been rain the night before and Joseph was eager to see if the moisture had coaxed any of the wheat that had been planted to take root and start growing.

Seventeen

Dreams

"I know what your concerns are, Mary. I was there when the boy was born. I remember scrambling to Egypt one step ahead of Herod's butcher boys. I know why we're in Nazareth," Joseph said as his wife rested her head on his chest.

"The angel said that he was the Son of God and that he would save us all from our sins. I can't begin to understand what that all means. What I do know is that every time we have thought to bring Jesus to Judea, God Himself has stopped us," said Mary.

"Let's stop talking about it for the night, Mary. If God doesn't want us to bring him down to Jerusalem, He will surely send a messenger in my dreams before we go. Besides, God knows that if the boy is to be a proper man of Israel and be accepted in our culture, he will have to go to the temple sometime. Maybe this year is better than next? We must trust God that He has his hand on the boy." Pulling his wife closer to him and hugging her, trying to sooth her fears which, he knew, were the same fears he had, Joseph slowly drifted off to sleep, thinking of animal mangers, eastern lords, and the burial tombs he had seen while down in Egypt.

Eighteen

A Decision Is Made

Tuesday morning dawned with great expectation for Mary and Joseph. God had never before failed to provide clear guidance for them in regard to Jesus and they expected that this time would not be any different. Joseph awoke to find Mary already up, as was usual for a wife and mother of a large family. He rose to a sitting position as the first beams of light from the rising sun shown through the window that faced to the east. "Mary must have opened the shutters when she got up," thought Joseph as he got up to put on his tunic. While he dressed, he searched his memory for any hint that he might have dreamed the night before and been given a message. The fact that he had not had that kind of a dream in over nine years did not lesson the fact that when God's messenger spoke, a person was likely never to forget the experience.

Satisfying himself that no message had been proffered through his dreams, Joseph went off in search of Mary. As he pulled the blanket away from the opening that led out into the family area that held the dinning table and reclining cushions, Joseph smelled a wonderful aroma. He knew that this morning he would be served eggs for breakfast, his and Jesus' favorite meal for that time of the morning.

Mary settled down onto her cushion for a quick bite with her family after attending the children. Joseph noticed that she would not look him in the eye and wondered what that meant. After 13 years of marriage, Joseph still could not read every mood of his wife, nor could he predict with any measure of success her reaction to any situation. He had learned to prepare himself for any eventuality, though the result of looking at life like that could be, at times, very stressful.

Joseph finally stopped his wife after the children had run off to either play or to their assigned chores and before she could begin to clean off the table and escape into the daily chores that would end only at the time of death. "What's the big secret, Mary?" asked Joseph with a serious look accentuated with a furrowed brow.

Mary put down the empty plates that had held the eggs and finally looked Joseph squarely in the eye. "I was awakened last night soon after we had both gone to sleep," she said, with a gleam in her eyes he recognized at once as having had an experience with God Himself. "A voice calling my name woke me up and told me to stand by the window in our bedchamber that faced east." As if remembering it for the first time, she looked up at Joseph and said, "I think I forgot to close it this morning, was it still open when you awoke?"

"Yes it was. I had to wrap a sheet around myself until I could close the shutters," said Joseph.

"Any way, when I got to the window last night, I opened the shutters and as I looked out at the stars, it seemed like the whole sky was split open. I saw the Temple as it sits on the mountaintop, as if looking through it. It's hard to describe. When I looked towards the Holy Place it seemed like I could look right in. If what I saw was correct, then everything in there was exactly like it says it should be in the Law of Moses. The seven headed menorah candle stand shown brightly and, as I approached the curtain separating the place I was at from the Holy of Holies, I noticed that I was alone, that no priest was present. I could sense a presence behind the veil and wondered how the priest could work in a place that was so awe inspiring – I could not utter a word, much less move. Just then, the veil started to rip, from the top to the bottom and an incredibly bright light shown through where the rending was. As I turned my head away, not wanting to look at God in His glory, I heard the same voice that had awakened me earlier. "Mary, do not be afraid to take the boy to Jerusalem. I have ordained this time for the boy, and he will soon come to understand what I have prepared for him."

"I was both afraid and overjoyed that our Lord had spoken to me," said Mary, now looking directly in his eyes. "Before the sky closed back up and the stars were all there was to see, I saw one more thing in the Temple." Walking toward Joseph while never taking her eyes from his, she reached for his hands and then told him the rest. "Before the vision ended, I was compelled to look back, into the Holy of Holies."

Joseph sucked in his breath as the ramification of his wife's statement struck home. "How is it that you're alive? No one has seen God and lived."

"When I looked back, I tell you Joseph, I could not help it, what I saw was both at once wonderful and very confusing. I saw the bright form of God, but His presence didn't sear my mind because there was someone standing between him and me. It was Jesus, our son, Joseph. Jesus was standing between God and me, a torn end of the veil in each of his hands. It was as if Jesus was standing in the gap, protecting me from the very Holy presence of God," explained Mary.

"Then we are to take the boy with us this year?" asked Joseph who was still processing the other information that his wife had given him.

"Yes, we are," said Mary. "What do you make of the rest of the vision?"

"I don't know Mary. It seems that the boy is just a boy except when God talks to us. Whatever He has planned for Jesus, it is beyond us."

Nineteen

Hats At the Table

As Joseph got up from the table to leave for the council fire, he reached for the special yarmulke that he wore when he went to the nightly meeting. As he reached into the wood box were he stored such things, he came out with not only his but also another one, exactly like it. Walking back over to the table, he looked at Jesus and silently handed to Jesus the twin head covering.

Jesus looked at the yarmulke and a smile slowly crept over his face. "Does this mean I can go to Passover this year?" he asked.

"The moment you are confirmed in the Temple by the High Priest of Israel, you will be required to never be without your covering. Until next month when that happens, keep the hat as a promise that God Himself wants you to join Him in the Passover Celebration in His Holy Temple." With that Joseph turned and walked out the door and went down the stairs. Jesus turned – he couldn't remember when he had stood up – and moved to hug his mother, tears streaming down his eyes in happiness otherwise reserved only for his nightly visits with His Heavenly Father.

Twenty

Roadside Emergency

The woman was stumbling and could not keep up. She and her husband, Raul, had set out from Tarsus, a city on the coast in the providence of Cilicia, thinking they had time to get to Jerusalem before she would deliver, but the baby was coming *now*.

Raul had wanted the baby, his first, to be born in Jerusalem. He was the leading Pharisee in the port city of Tarsus and his best friend was now the greatest teacher of the Jewish faith in all of Judaism. His friend, Gamaliel – also from Tarsus – was teaching and doing research in Jerusalem at the Temple. Raul wanted Gamaliel to be present at the circumcision of his son. "If the child is a boy," thought Raul, who then said a prayer. "Oh God, please let it be a boy."

Leah had started her labor when the ship that had taken them from Tarsus to Tyre had been in sight of the port. Raul had rushed Leah off the boat as soon as it landed at the once magnificent city famous for its cedar trees. Leah told Raul as soon as they had departed the ship that the pains had stopped. Not knowing the nature of labor pains, Raul had immediately started out for Ptolemais, about 10 miles south of Tyre. About halfway to Ptolemais, on the coast road, Leah went into labor for real. Raul was walking quickly, wanting to get to the town before darkness fell.

"I think we can make it," said Raul, turning to his wife only to find out she wasn't in stride with him. "It's just a couple of more miles up this road Looking around, he spotted her stopped in the middle of the road a few dozen feet behind him. "Leah," called Raul to his wife. "What's wrong?" Leah was breathing hard as Raul ran back to help her off to the side of the road. He noticed that her robe was soaking wet and realized that the baby was indeed coming soon, within the next couple of hours.

The couple had been traveling light, coming by boat to cut off most of the trip around the northwestern corner of the Great Sea. Raul had been counting on staying at Roman wayside inns that were ever present on the main roads throughout the empire. Without camping equipment and only having one change of clothing each, Raul knew that this night would be long, cold, and hard.

An hour into Leah's labor, Raul heard noise from the road. Assuring his wife that he would return in moment, Raul made his way up to the road to see who or what was making the noise. Coming up the road was a group of Roman soldiers. At the front of their marching formation was the company's centurion. Seeing Raul standing at the side of the road, the centurion, Gaius, called a halt to the march.

"Greetings from Rome in the name of Caesar and Mars," said the soldier as he pounded his breastplate with his clenched left hand. "Do you require any help?"

Returning the greeting, Raul told the centurion of his and his wife's predicament. "Do you have a physician in your troop?" asked Raul in desperation for his wife's condition.

"No," answered Gaius. "Only with the legions do physicians travel with the army. We do, however, have a medic-man. He has been taught how to sew up cuts and wounds, but not much more."

"Please call for him, I don't want my wife to die and it seems she is in great pain," said Raul, who would have taken a person with less knowledge and experience. The soon-to-be father had no experience with childbirth. This was his first child and when his mother had subsequent children after him, Raul had shown no interest in the goings on. As was common for most men of his generation, Raul was as ignorant of this particular human function as he was a brilliant scholar of the prophets of Jehovah.

A few minutes later, Gaius came back with a red headed soldier who looked far too young to march in the legions of Rome. "This is Rufus," introduced Gaius. "He says he can help."

"Come along now and show me where your wife is," said Rufus to Raul, in a voice that was too friendly for someone who wore a sword and held a spear. "You wouldn't know it to look at me, but I helped my own wife deliver our three children before our landlord decided I needed to become a soldier."

The baby came two hours later with Rufus cutting the cord and tying a less than perfect knot as close to the baby's stomach as possible.

"Look, madam, it is a boy," said Rufus who was busy cleaning the babe with his own red scarlet robe. The red headed soldier gave the baby a slap on the rear end to start the breathing process while he held the little boy by one ankle.

"Here," said Rufus as he handed the baby to its father. "I need to wait for the rest of it to come out and then we'll be done." Raul held up his son for his exhausted wife to see. He then said a prayer of thanksgiving for the gift of life he was holding. "Oh God of Abraham, please let this son live so that he can serve you as a teacher of your law," prayed Raul, knowing that one in four children died when born outside of the home or proper shelter.

Bundling the baby in his spare cloak and giving him to his mother to suckle, Raul sat next to his new family and prepared to keep watch while the two slept through the night. It was spring, the new moon and the month of Nisan, was only a week away. "We now have eight days to get to the temple for the naming, circumcision, and the sacrifice," said Raul out loud to himself. He counted it a blessing that there was no wind or rain tonight.

"The babe is born and appears to be healthy, sir," reported Rufus when he had walked back to the road to answer to the curious centurion.

"Good," said Gaius, who seemed pleased that he could offer any help in a situation like that one. "Was it a boy or girl?"

"A boy, sir," replied Rufus who then went on to make an observation. "It seemed to me that the babe had bowed legs, but I didn't say anything to the parents. Nothing you could do about it out here anyway."

"Very well, Rufus, you did well," said Gaius. "Go join the ranks. We'll be leaving in a few minutes."

"Yes, sir," barked Rufus, who then executed a perfect about face and walked back to his position I the formation. As Rufus rejoined the ranks, he was patted on the back and was semi-jokingly told that he was good for something. Gaius went off the road to see if there wasn't something else the troop could do for the traveling couple. He felt bad about leaving the new family there at the side of the road with no hope or way of getting to Ptolemais until the next day. In a way he could not quite grasp, he felt responsible for the newborn child and did not wish that any harm would come to it, if he had anything to do about it.

Approaching Raul, Gaius saw the couple sitting with their backs to a large tree, the babe sucking at his mother who glowed with fulfillment. Gaius also noticed that the mother looked like she could use a good night's rest. Turning back to the road and his troops, he ordered his squad leaders to order his men to set up camp. They would stay here for the night, with the traveling couple. Somehow, he felt responsible for this Jewish couple he had found on the road.

Twenty-One

All Roads Lead To Jerusalem

Later, that night, around a blazing fire in a clearing not far from where the birth of Raul and Leah's son had taken place, Gaius questioned Raul. "So how do you come to be on the road with your wife so pregnant?" asked Gaius. "Surely you knew she was close?"

"I knew she was close," answered Raul. "We just thought we could get to Jerusalem in time."

"In time for what?" asked Gaius, who could think of no good excuse to be on the road with a pregnant wife.

"I am a Pharisee of the Jewish religion," explained Raul. I am the Pharisee of Tarsus, as a matter of fact. Anyway, we wanted to get to Jerusalem in time for the Passover, which is not a problem. The problem is that we wanted to have our son born in Jerusalem. That is why we chanced it on the road."

"Why would you want that?" asked Gaius. "You're from Tarsus, which is a full Roman territory. Judea is only watched over from Rome. As it stands now, your son is a Roman citizen with full rights under the law of Caesar."

Raul had not thought of that, being born in Bethany, outside of Jerusalem. He had moved, shortly after his marriage, to be the rabbi in Tarsus at the behest of the chief priest. He thought it strange that his son was eligible for dual citizenship as both Roman and Jew.

"As soon as we get to Ptolemais, go to the town administrator and register your son's birth," Gaius said. "Have you named the lad yet?"

"No," said Raul. "According to Jewish custom, a male child is not named until the eighth day when he is also circumcised."

"I've never understood circumcision," said Gaius. "You should still register him, though."

"How can I register his birth for Roman citizenship tomorrow if I have no name to have recorded?" asked Raul of the centurion.

"I am leading the cohort to Jerusalem in a few days, after we rest from our journey from Rome in Ptolemais," said Gaius. "I will speak as a witness for you in front of the Roman consul in Jerusalem. If you come by the garrison that is by the Temple after your religious ritual, you will be able to find me there." The night passed in more comfort that Raul and Leah could have hoped. A tent was provided to them by the soldiers and was set up close to the fire which was kept burning all night. The babe and his mother slept a peaceful night.

The next day, the couple with their military escort entered the town of Ptolemais and found a room at the Roman hostel called the Inn of the Goat. There the couple stayed for two days, while Leah regained her energy and their son, who would be named at his circumcision, grew strong and gained a more pinkish color from the bluish tint that he was born with.

The couple joined a caravan heading south to Jerusalem for Passover when they set out again. It would take four days to reach the Temple City, which pleased Raul. His son would be circumcised and dedicated to God during

Passover and he would spend that religious holiday at the home of his now famous friend. Two Roman centuries that were rotating accompanied the caravan, to Raul's surprise, to Jerusalem as part of the occupation force from Rome. At their head marched the centurion Gaius, who asked about the health of Leah and the baby before attending to the troops under his charge.

Raul felt torn traveling with the soldiers. On the one hand, he was glad for the protection for his wife and son from the roving bands of robbers and thieves that seemed to roam the middle section of this war torn land. Samaria teemed with dangers for the unwary traveler. On the other had, it was Rome that was slowly taking over this land with the all-important temple. Raul said a prayer for God to send his Messiah to free His people from the awful oppression. He prayed that his son should know and help the Messiah to sweep the land and set up His throne.

As Raul prayed, he felt a peace come over him, the like of which he had never known before. He felt that still small voice that seemed to emanate from his heart and not his head, tell him that his prayer would be answered. As Raul prayed, the soldiers moved into position to march behind the caravan. As they passed by Raul, he waved to Rufus. Rufus for his part, smiled as he passed. If he had waved back, he was sure Gaius would have punished him for breaking discipline.

Twenty-Two

A Caravan is Spared

Nidel stared at the caravan coming down the road from his perch 100 feet up the side of a sheer cliff that overhung the winding mountain path. He was the lookout for a group of 20 men who had taken to the hills and mountains three years before, after a drought had made them forfeit their fields and lands to Jewish moneylenders. Now the group preyed on Jewish travelers, relieving them of their riches and sometimes their lives. For most of the thieves in Nidel's band, the evictions of three years ago had been the second time in the last sixty years that they and their descendents had been forcibly deprived of their lands. The first time was when Herod the Great had come to power. He had moved some Jews from Judea to the northern part of Samaria, now called Galilee. In order for the Jews to inherit the land, those who worked the land already were told to go away.

The thieves hated the Galilean Jews for the theft of their land and had no qualms in returning the favor as the faithful traveled south to Jerusalem three times a year to sacrifice. Nidel was about to whistle the bird-song sounding code accompanied by a wave of his hand that would set an ensuing ambush in motion when he saw the glint of metal reflected by the sun. Sucking in the breath that he was about to let loose in the whistle, he waited to see what the sun had flashed on.

As the caravan drew closer, he saw that what had caught his eye were the raised spears of the Roman guards marching behind the travelers. Nidel had almost made a huge mistake. Had he given the signal, his fellow thieves would have been slaughtered. Better, he thought to let this caravan pass. He knew that more than three others would be passing by in the next day, as Passover was near. With that decision made, Nidel moved away from the ledge that was his spy perch and moved down the opposite side of the cliff to confer with his partners. He needed to tell them to stay away from the road for the next hour or so while the guarded caravan passed.

Nidel and his comrades had not forgotten their friends, Thaddeus, Muckel and Treype. It had only been a few months since the three had attacked a small caravan only to run into Roman soldiers. While Muckel and Treype had given up immediately upon being caught by the sneaky Roman guard who had disguised themselves as pilgrims on the road, Thaddeus had fought back and in his struggle, had managed to kill one soldier and wound two more. By all rights, he should have died on the spot from a thrown javelin or arrow but one of the soldiers had sneaked up behind him in the fight and clubbed him with a shield.

Later, Nidel had seen, from his perch that he had just left, the wood beams threaded through the arms and across the back of each of the three thieves heads. Their fate was not left to the imagination. He had last seen them being marched away to the north, no doubt going to Sepphoris for trial and execution.

Nidel had no illusion that such a fate might await him one day. All he wanted was for his boy, now just turning five years of age, to have a better chance at a good life. If robbing a few hated Jews was how fate let him provide toward that future, so be it. He looked up to the sky and prayed, ironically, to the same God that the Jews themselves worshiped, "Oh Lord, please strengthen my hand so that my son will have a chance." With that prayer, Nidel struggled to his feet and headed back to his lookout perch. Another caravan would be making its way through the pass soon. Perhaps, he thought, that one will be without a Roman Legion guard attached to it.

Had Nidel stayed at his perch after he spotted the guards, he would have seen Raul, Leah and their son pass beneath his hiding place on their way to the temple and to their friend Gamaliel's house where they could rest from the hard travels. He might or might not have seen Rufus, along with other young men in the cohort, dressed up like travelers, walking out in front of the caravan in a classic disguised point maneuver. Raul had prayed earlier for traveling mercies. He would never know that his prayer had been answered.

Twenty-Three

Caravan Crossroads

The week before his yearly Passover trip to Jerusalem was always a busy one for Joseph. Most of the Jewish travelers that made the trip from Galilee formed their caravans in Nazareth. For the small town's carpenter, that meant days filled with repairs to wagons and hitches.

In the weeks following the decision to include Jesus in the trip, the young apprentice had assumed more and more duties in the carpenter's shop. Because of the professional and skillful way the boy had handled the Torah chest project, Joseph more and more left the lad alone to complete the projects that were assigned to him. Because of the addition of the added craftsman, Joseph found that he was able to complete the jobs given him more quickly and therefore be able to take on all the more. Business that year was very good and Joseph was quick to thank God for his oldest boy.

As the family loaded up their cart, the one usually used for deliveries, Joseph did a mental inventory of what they would need for the coming two weeks. The trip usually took three days. By the middle of the first day, they would be climbing the Samarian mountain passes and would camp by a Roman outpost that night, near the ancient city of Samaria, built at the time when Israel had been split apart by internal dissent hundreds of years before. Ten of the twelve tribes that had formed the nation under Kings David and Solomon had broken away and formed a new, northern nation called Israel. The southern kingdom of two tribes had kept its capital at Jerusalem and had called itself Judah.

The second day would see the caravan come down out of the foothills, where again they would camp by another Roman outpost. The last day would see them pass around the town of Emmaus and start the climb to the Holy City. The caravan that Joseph and his family would join with consisted mostly of distant family members and friends from Nazareth and the surrounding area. There were some fishermen from the Sea of Galilee that would also go with them. Joseph had worked on some of their boats from time to time, years before when he had to go abroad to find work. He knew them to be gruff men who had led tough, difficult lives, but for all that, honest and hard working and good to have along on a dangerous trip.

Reports had filtered in over the last few weeks that the gangs of thieves that were robbing caravans had lessened their activities with the capture and crucifixion of the criminals that had been executed in Nazareth the month before. The men who had taken this trip every year knew that would not last long. Joseph was more concerned this year than in years past. Mary had stayed up north every since they had come back from Egypt because of his and Mary's reluctance to take Jesus into Judea. Joseph had made the yearly trip because that was what was required of all Jewish males. Now the whole family was going and for him, the responsibility was that much greater.

Inspecting the cart and supplies for the last time, Joseph gave Jesus the high sign to guide the donkey toward the road leading south. Whispering a prayer for safety on the road, he took hold of his wife's hand and started the first journey he had taken with her in more than nine years.

Twenty-Four

Through the Passes of Samaria

Nidel scanned the road from his lookout perch and spotted the dust rising from the caravan as it neared the mountain pass where his gang laid in wait. As the group got closer, he could see that many more families were involved in this traveling troupe than in the last one. He considered that might be a good indication of whether there were soldiers present, as good Jewish parents would not want to let their children roam and play with the hardened legionnaires present.

Children played as the carts and wagons moved along and Nidel was sure that no Roman guard accompanied this particular caravan. Usually, the travelers – especially those with children present – were easy targets. The gang would be on them in a moment and a knock to the head of the biggest of the men would subdue any thought of fighting. Members of the gang could then go through the possessions of the travelers, find any hidden money and valuables that were inevitably hidden in the "same" secret locations time and time again and be off in less than 10 minutes. Some of the time, if the caravan was big enough, they would wait for the first half to pass in the narrow road of the mountain pass and then hold up the second half and have more time to be thorough in their search.

Rarely did any of the travelers have to be killed or injured beyond a knot on the head that would serve to teach a needed lesson. While the Jews and the mixed Samaritan and displaced Jewish robbers hated each other, each knew that a fight would do neither of them any good. Besides, thought Nidel, killing and maiming would only bring the Roman soldiers in greater numbers and none of his compatriots felt like being hunted down like wild animals.

Nidel looked one last time as the caravan passed under his ridge. When he saw nothing untoward, he signaled by simply throwing a rock to the other side of the ravine, sounding out his bird-song whistle and giving a pre-arranged arm wave. Moments after his signal, 20 desperate-looking men, along with five boys and three women, appeared as if out of nowhere on either side of the road, brandishing clubs, hammers and short knives. As one person they fell on the 200-person caravan, stopping it in place and creating panic and dismay.

Twenty-Five

Fighting, Biting, and Hooking

Joseph and his family quickly got into a monotonous routine inside the first couple of hours of being on the road. Joseph, Jesus or James would lead the donkey and cart while Mary would walk along side the cart that carried their youngest set of twins and the provisions for the trip. Miriam and the other children took turns alternating from running and playing amongst the other members of the caravan and resting in the cart while helping their mother with the younger kids.

Miriam had found a couple of young girls her own age that were daughters of one of the fisherman that had joined their traveling party. Zephora and Saphira were the daughters of Zebudee, a successful fisherman who owned several boats and worked and lived about half way down the shoreline of the Sea of Galilee on the Galilean side.

Zephora and Miriam had much in common in that both had younger sets of twin brothers, they were the same age and were looking for an excuse not to be around their respective families. Neither wanted to 'play' mama on a trip such as this one and they knew that their mothers would quickly put them to work if they showed their faces too often around the traveling carts that had become their moving houses.

The two young ladies were walking along the side of the road near the front of the caravan, looking for unusual rocks, when they saw the gang of rough looking thugs coming from behind the trees and running straight for them. Even at the age that they were, both young girls knew outlaws when they saw them and immediately began screaming in terror and fright, both frozen to where they stood, unable to move at all.

Lucius, leader of the gang, was the first of the men to reach the girls. He quickly clamped a hand over each of their mouths as soon as he reached them. Surprise was the greatest weapon his men had and while the girls were not that far away from the main body of the caravan, they were far enough away to alert a resistance that could prove costly in terms of time, money and manpower. As he considered all of these things, he felt a searing pain in the palm of his right hand and yanking it back, let out a long abusive curse.

Once she had freed herself from Lucius's hand, Miriam let out a bloodcurdling scream that only a nine-year-old girl could do. More panicked than frightened, she kept screaming as Lucius tried to calm her down. What had panicked the hysterical girl was not the presence of the outlaw by itself, but the fact that when he had clamped his hand over her mouth he had inadvertently also covered her nostrils. When Miriam came to the point of not being able to breathe, she had lashed out in any way she could to get a breath. Joseph and Mary both heard their daughter scream at the same time.

"That sounds like Miriam," said Mary, who had heard the same scream many times before.

"I'll go and see what's gotten into her," said Joseph who also had no doubt about the source of the scream. "Look, the caravan is stopping. Joseph took off running toward the sound of his daughter's scream and as soon as he cleared the center of the caravan recognized exactly what was taking place.

A scrawny, malnourished man a good four inches shorter than Joseph came running at him, swinging a large, heavy oak tree branch that had been carved into club. The fact that Joseph recognized what kind of wood the man was swinging at his head almost made him stop and laugh. As if he didn't have enough on his mind. Just then he saw Miriam being backhanded by a man sucking his other hand in his mouth. Joseph felt the blood boil in his veins and then he saw red. Some inhuman monster was attacking his daughter and nothing or no one was going to get in his way of helping her.

Stepping inside the swing of the scrawny man swinging the heavy oak club was child's play for the rugged, well-fed carpenter as he snatched the club out of mid-air and threw the scrawny man into a thorn bush all in one motion. Running straight for Lucius, Joseph never took his eyes off the man who had struck his daughter. He didn't notice the veins that had begun to pop up all over his forehead and the back of his hands.

Back at the donkey, Jesus realized that their caravan was under attack. Seeing his father run off to find Miriam, he immediately anchored the mule so that it would not run away by rolling a large rock over the rope he had been leading it by. Finished with that, he had run back to his mother and seeing that she was momentarily okay, dived into the back of the cart.

Jesus quickly rounded up James and both sets of twins after he emerged from the cart gathered them together at the cart. "James, help Mother get the rest of the children under the cart," Jesus said. "I'll stand lookout until Dad gets back."

"I can help you fight," said James, who didn't want to hide with his Mother and siblings.

"I need you to stay with mother!" said Jesus sharply to his younger brother. "I don't have time to argue with you, just do it." Jesus stood sentry over his family gripping and re-gripping a large hammer. The carpenters used the hammer for driving the large pegs that would secure the family's tent when they stopped for the night. Soon, bandits started coming by but upon seeing the young boy with the large hammer would pass by the cart in search of less dangerous fair. Jesus only once had to swing the hammer at someone. A boy about his age, whose name was Sidel bar Nidel, waved a knife at the carpenter's apprentice.

"So, little man has a hammer, does he?" said Sidel to Jesus. "If you wave that hammer at me one more time, I'll take it from you and slit you top to bottom." Jesus said nothing to the young thief but neither did he drop the hammer. "Too good to talk to me little man?" asked Sidel. "Well, you just stay there while I get what I came for." The young thief started for the back of the cart when Jesus once more swung the hammer to keep the boy away.

"Go away," said Jesus, whose mouth was suddenly dry. "You're not getting near this wagon."

Sidel smiled as he came closer to Jesus with the knife held low. "Can't say I didn't warn you," he said. The two boys prepared to fight when a loud shout was heard coming form the front of the caravan. Sidel stopped when he heard the sound.

"Maybe another day," Sidel said. "You need to learn that a hammer is no good in a knife fight."

Jesus dropped the hammer with both excitement and fear when he saw the boy run off. "Is every one alright?"

Jesus asked his family. "We're fine," answered Mary. "Have you seen your father or Miriam?" "No," said Jesus who picked up the hammer and turned to face out from the cart again. "Just stay there until they get back."

Twenty-Six

Consequences

Joseph ran toward the coward who had hit Miriam and taking one last long stride, hit the man squarely on the head with the club he had acquired from the short and scrawny man. Lucius only had time to turn around before the carpenter was all over him, and the last thing he heard before passing out was the keening of the little girl that had bitten a chunk out of his hand.

Joseph immediately snatched up Miriam after discarding the club and putting a hand out for Zephora started back for the center of the caravan. A shout went up behind him and he saw the other bedraggled men, women and boys running back into the brush and boulders, some carrying objects of value, some empty-handed, and others holding various injuries to arms, torsos and heads.

Joseph felt Zephora's hand leave his own as they passed by her father's wagon. Zebudee broke out into an audible sigh of relief when he saw the carpenter let go of the little girl so she could return to her family. The big fisherman was brandishing a wicked looking hook that Joseph had seen other people in the same business use to retrieve full nets of fish. Joseph also noticed the man lying at the fisherman's feet and the blood dripping from the hook. "At least one of the barbarians would not be going home, wherever that was, tonight," Joseph thought.

Coming back to his own cart, Joseph found Jesus standing guard over the rest of the family. The boy had the giant peg hammer in his hands. The carpenter also noticed that the hands that held the hammer were shaking. Releasing the sobbing Miriam to Mary who was climbing out from under the cart, Joseph walked up to Jesus and took the hammer out of his hand. "You did well Jesus, are you hurt at all?" asked a proud father who once again was out of breath.

"Only one of them attacked me and I held him off long enough before they all ran away," answered Jesus, who was also out of breath and equally red in the face, and shivering like he had just got out of a river in mid-winter. After a quick check and meeting by all of the family leaders, it was decided to post sentries and to move on as quickly as they could. Some of the older men shook their head in disgust and berated themselves for not doing so before. "It's not like a quick trip to the sea," they said.

Only one of the robbers had been killed, the one Zebudee had felled with his boat hook. They left him on the side of the road, making sure not to touch him. Passover was within a week and none of the group wanted to have to wait an additional month to celebrate because a dead person had made them unclean.

Soon the caravan was over the highest peak and headed down into the valley where they would camp for the night. On arriving at the camping spot set aside for caravans just like this one, the elders of the group made their way to the Roman outpost and reported the attack. "Our caravan was attacked just a couple of hours ago," said one of the elders to the centurion on duty. "One of the thieves is up on the road dead."

"Yes, yes," said the centurion with a yawn. "You're not the first. It's being handled by the legions. We catch criminals every day."

"Some of our valuables were stolen," continued the elder. "If you find them, how do we get them back?"

"You don't," laughed the centurion. "If you want them back, go into the mountains and get them back yourselves." The elders left with this answer, suspecting that the legionnaires kept whatever booty they recovered. With the most dangerous part of the journey over with, the people of the caravan enjoyed the fresh air of camping out. The tents went up quickly and the women were soon cooking over open fires in the cool spring air.

Jesus walked a short distance from the camp to hold his nightly prayer meeting with himself and God as the participants. He was very confused about how he had acted that day when confronted with personal harm and threats to his family. That someone of his own group should have been the deliverer of deadly violence and knowing that he had been prepared to protect his family with the same kind of action troubled the young apprentice at the core. The violence made him nauseous; that he had been so close to taking human life himself almost stopped his breath. He was still shaking, not from fear of what the robbers threatened, but from fear of what he almost did. People died every day in the world around him. It was part of life, part of God's plan. But when someone died from violence he knew it was not part of life, not part of God's plan, even if it was that person's fault.

Sitting down for a long talk with his God, Jesus started weeping for the men who had attacked them. They seemed so desperate and needful. Yet he knew that what they sought, revenge and 'things', would never satisfy their needs. Only God could do that.

Twenty-Seven

In Need of Direction

The young boy sat looking at the fire as if he could look into the heart of God Himself. Tears ran freely down his cheeks as he tried to face up to the fact that his father was dead. His mother had died the year before at the hands of drunken Roman legionnaires who had found her alone while she was looking for food to feed him and his father. Now his father was gone too, and the boy knew what it was like to be totally alone in an angry world.

Looking up at Lucius, who was trying without much success to comfort the grieving boy who would soon be 14 years of age, Barabbas asked the leader of thieves what had gone wrong.

"Some of the others saw what happened to your father," said Lucius, who then put on a wry smile. "I of course didn't see a thing, when that mad man with the club tried to spill my brains out." Taking a deep breath, Lucius continued. "Your father was holding up a large man. You know that we usually go for the biggest first. Well, anyway, apparently the man was a fisherman. Before your father could tap him on the head, he came up swinging some kind of giant hook. The fisherman caught him in the neck and that was that."

Fresh tears streamed down the face of young Barabbas as he took this in. First the Romans, he thought and now Jewish Galileans. Curse them both, he thought. Looking up once more at Lucius, Barabbas asked, "What about me now? Do I have to leave the gang and go to relatives or can I stay?"

Feeling responsible for the boy's problems and misery, Lucius put an arm around the orphan and pulled him to his self. "I will take care of you," the gang leader said. "You are a part of this gang."

Giving an oath to both himself and to Lucius, Barabbas said, "I will never fail you Lucius. I will become the best robber and thief. Together, we will hunt down both Jew and Roman."

Lucius looked cautiously at the young boy whose eyes shined with the thought of revenge. "Barabbas, be careful. I rob people to get their money, not because I hold a personal hatred for any one of them. Remember that your mother was a Jew, and so, by their laws, you are one too. Do you want to ravage, kill, and steal from your own family and blood?"

"I will do anything to avenge my father and mother's blood," said grief-stricken boy. "I have no other family but who I see around this fire. I will die before I let a Jew or Roman show me a kindness."

When Lucius looked up from the steely eyed young boy, he saw Sidel making his way around the fire to where they were both sitting. Nodding his head at the lookout's oldest boy, the leader of the gang got up and walked away. He would himself, this very night, go back to the pass under cover of darkness and bury his friend and colleague. No one deserved to have the birds eat their flesh until the bones showed, he thought. Not even if that person was a thief.

Twenty-Eight

Behold the City

The caravan ran into no more problems for the next couple of days. The nights were festive as the women were allowed to come around the nightly fire, along with the men. The children accompanied their mothers around the flames and were in awe as their fathers and other elders made decisions on the way the trip was being traveled. Inventories had been taken and the losses from the attack had for the most part been minimal. A few of the men had knots on their heads from being struck from behind during the attack.

The night before, the group from Nazareth had spent the night on the outskirts of Emmaus. As each family cleaned up from the morning's breakfast and prepared to make the final journey, the sun started its climb into the sky from the general direction in which they were headed.

Jerusalem was a city set on a hill. Approaching it from any angle required a steady climb from below sea level to more than 3,000 feet. While most of the families in the caravan had carts or wagons drawn by donkeys or oxen, the transports were mostly for the very young, very old or for the supplies that would sustain them for the two weeks that they would be gone from their homes.

The people of the caravan caught their first glimpse of Jerusalem as they rounded a bend in the mountain road. As the men and women pointed out to the children the

Temple that sat high above the city proper, the group itself picked up the pace at the anticipation of the end of the journey. Jesus, who was leading the donkey cart, looked up at the Temple as they drew closer to the City of David. 'The Temple of God,' Jesus thought to himself.

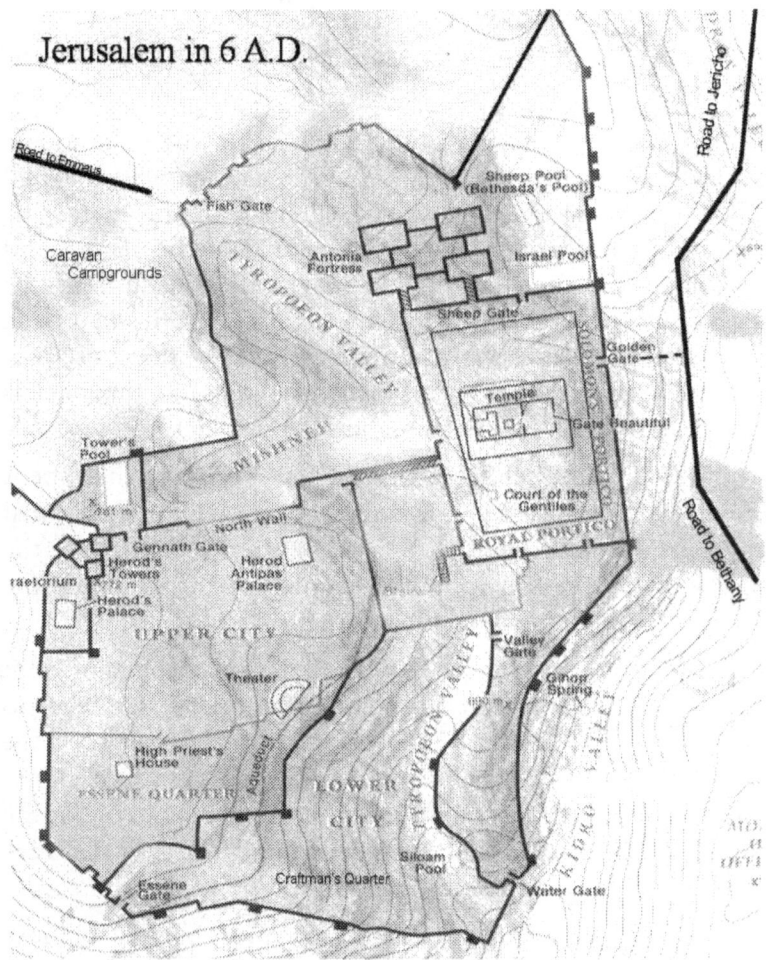

According to what he had learned in the Chronicles of the Kings, as recorded by scribes like Ezra, Jesus remembered that it was on this site that he was looking at that God had descended on the Holy of Holies in the time of Solomon and dwelt among His people. The draw that he felt was indescribable. He felt a sense of being home that was unlike anything he had ever felt in Nazareth. Mary came up from behind her oldest son and observed his reaction to the Temple and the Holy City.

"You have been here before, Jesus," said Mary, as she took his left arm and walked with him. "You were eight days old when we, your dad and I, came up from Bethlehem and presented you at this very Temple for circumcision and for me to pay the ransom due for the birth of a male child."

"It feels like home to me," said Jesus, to his mother as he continued to look at the great city that had been in existence almost as long as Jericho. "I can't explain it, but I feel as if I would do anything for the people that live here."

"I don't know what to tell you about what your feeling, my son," said Mary, looking intently at the wonder in his face. "I do think that soon we will have to have a talk about some of the things that have happened before, during, and right after the time you were born. Not now though and certainly not here," said Mary, as once more she remembered the horrors of the night and the days that followed when she and Joseph fled to Egypt with Jesus. "Let's try and not think of those things now and enjoy the rest of the trip. We will talk again of this when we get home. This should be a happy time for all of us. I have not been here myself since I presented you twelve years ago and I, also, look forward to going to the Temple to worship in the court of women."

Mary left Jesus' side and went back to attend to the small children who always seemed to need looking after. While everyone considered the two set of twins to be a blessing sent from God Himself, the task of looking after them – especially outside of the home – was a chore that took most of the energy right out of her.

"Where is Miriam when I need her? Or for that matter, James?" Mary said to herself. "You would think that girl would be scared to death to even leave the wagon after what she went through." It had only taken one night for the girl and her brother to decide that it was safe to roam about freely again. Mary thought to herself that Miriam might have become timid after her encounter with the thief, but the young got over traumas quickly and perhaps that was the way God had intended children to be. If they remembered everything in its horror, they would end up not doing anything.

The caravan came to the campgrounds outside of the gates of Jerusalem one hour after noon. The flat area, set on a large hill top inside the ancient walls of the city when it was at its peak in the time of Kings David and Solomon, was already filling up as caravans like their own climbed the mountain and started preparations for the coming Passover.

Joseph and Mary had talked about going on to Bethlehem, a half day's journey from Jerusalem and staying a few days with Mary's relatives and letting them see Jesus again. It had been twelve years since the couple had struggled in that night with Mary clearly in labor and finding that the upper floors of the guesthouse were already full. Mary's cousins had delighted in holding the babe, even after shepherds had made their way to the place that he had been born. Joseph's relatives also lived in Bethlehem and had come over after the son of one of those shepherds ran across town to let them know their northern relatives had just made it to town before their first born had come into the world.

The carpenter and his wife had decided against making the trip farther south. The Lord had told Mary that Jerusalem would be safe for Jesus. He had said nothing about Bethlehem and that was the place where they had run from all those years ago.

Twenty-Nine

Cousins of Destiny

The afternoon before Passover was always a special time for those pilgrims who had to travel from various parts of the world to Jerusalem. It was a time of reunion for families that only got to see each other once a year. Not only did Jesus get to experience Jerusalem for the first time but he also met relatives that had seldom or never visited Galilee.

"So we must be cousins?" asked John, who was the same age as the carpenter's apprentice. "I've heard about you from my mother. How come you've never come down with them for Passover in the past?"

"I've always stayed behind with the older grandmothers of my town, who can no longer travel," said Jesus, who was delighted to finally meet his cousin who was only a couple of months older than he. "How come your parents and family have never come north to visit? My mother also has talked about you and your mother. She tells me they were together a lot when they were pregnant with us."

"I was born in the hill country of Judah, but right after I was named and circumcised my father Zacharias was transferred to Jericho," said John. Both boys were sitting on some large boulders that had been used for outer walls in the distant past. "My father died when I was about five and mom decided to stay there."

"I remember my father leaving suddenly for Jericho and my mother being very sad," said Jesus. "She couldn't go with him to your father's funeral because she was pregnant and due with the first set of twins."

"From the look of your hands I would guess you are apprenticed to your father to be a carpenter," said John, who still missed his father and was at times uncomfortable talking about the former priest of the Temple. "Don't you wish you could be something else?"

"I've never thought about it," said Jesus with a wrinkled forehead as he contemplated doing something else with his life. "I've always liked working with wood and I'm now starting to get my own paying jobs."

"My mother wants me to follow my father and be a priest at the Temple," said John with a shake of his head. "Have you been up there yet? Most of those serving before the Lord wouldn't know His voice if He stood next to them in the flesh like He did with Abraham."

"So what to you want to do?" asked Jesus. "Most boys our age are already apprenticed and in training. Wait too long and you'll end up a vagabond with no skills."

"I feel like God wants me to serve Him in a different way," said John with a quiet intensity. "Like how Samuel or maybe even Elijah served Him. I'm called to be a prophet, Jesus. Like the prophets of old except that there hasn't been men and women like that in Israel in over 400 years."

"Well, I can't tell you what to do, but I will tell you this," said Jesus equally serious and intense. "If you are hearing God correctly, He will lead you to what is right in His sight. Has He told you anything about what He will have you say or do?"

"I have had dreams of baptizing people in the Jordan, kind of like what Elisha did with that leper," said John. "I've dreamed of being in the desert alone, yet with thousands of people coming and going." Turning to look at Jesus in the eye and standing up, the last thing the son of his mother's best friend said shook Jesus to his core. "I see the Messiah every night I lay down to sleep. I see him coming to me in the desert." The mood was broken as Mary called to the boys for the noon meal.

"My mother and I are leaving for Jericho the morning after Passover," said John. "I hope it will be less than twelve years before we see each other again. In the mean time it will be nice to hang out with someone my own age. Have you noticed the lack of boys our age around here?" Jesus nodded his head in agreement as the two walked back to the family's encampment. He liked this long-lost cousin. Somehow he knew that John talked with God just as he himself did and that made the carpenter's son feel good in a way he didn't understand.

Thirty

Passover

Six-year-old Rachel stood up and drew a big breath. The pavilion tent was brightly lit and she could see the faces, both familiar and strange all looking at her, some with broad smiles on their faces and some with serious looks of expectation. Her big brother, Jesus, had practiced with her all day long and while a little timid because of the strangers, she felt confident that she could do this.

Even though Lydia and she were the same age, Rachel was the youngest by more than an hour and technically was not even born on the same day. Mary had given birth to Lydia before the sun had set and then again to Rachel after the new day had started. Because of all these things, Rachel, as the youngest child who could speak, could participate in this year's Passover celebration.

Taking another big breath, the little girl began, "Why is this night different from all others?" Smiling at the little girl, Joseph's uncle Bartholomew, who had come up to celebrate the Passover from Bethlehem, rose from his seat at the head of the table and began the formal answer as was his right, honor and privilege as the most elder family member present.

"This night is different because it was on this night many years ago that God delivered His people out of bondage to the Egyptians," said Bartholomew. Spread out before them was a large roasted lamb that would be eaten before the night was over. No one would sleep that night, but stories of how God delivered His people and the many miracles that He had done would be recalled deep into the night as everyone present ate until the lamb was completely consumed. The lamb was to be eaten along with unleavened bread and a mixture of herbs. The bread was flat and had little taste, so the herb mixture helped in the eating. The roasted lamb had been prepared earlier in the day after being blessed by the High Priest at the Temple. It had been cooking ever since, and since others in the city were doing the same thing, the aroma had set everyone's appetite on a fine edge.

At around midnight, the family and extended family of Joseph and Mary were silent. It had been a few minutes since the last story was told and now guarded glances between the men signaled that all of the 'regular' stories and traditions had been taken care of. Just then a young teenage voice sounded just to the right of Joseph. The carpenter just had time to turn his head when he saw his son, Jesus, stand and start to tell a story. Joseph was shocked when he recognized the text and realized that his son was again quoting the Holy words of the Torah. The boy started in a whisper and then his voice grew louder with confidence and he lost himself in the recitation.

> *"And the Lord said unto Moses, carve for yourself two tables of stone like unto the first: and I will write upon these tables the words that were in the first tables, which you broke.*
> *And be ready in the morning, and come up in the morning unto Mount Sinai, and present yourself there to me in the top of the mount.*
> *And no man shall come up with thee, neither let any man be seen throughout the entire mount; neither let the flocks nor herds feed before that mount.*

And he hewed two tables of stone like unto the first; and Moses rose up early in the morning, and went up unto mount Sinai, as the Lord had commanded him, and took in his hand the two tables of stone.

And the Lord descended in the cloud, and stood with him there, and proclaimed the name of the Lord.

And the Lord passed by before him, and proclaimed, The Lord, The Lord God, merciful and gracious, longsuffering, and abundant in goodness and truth,

Keeping mercy for thousands, forgiving iniquity and transgression and sin, and that will by no means clear the guilty; visiting the iniquity of the fathers upon the children, and upon the children's children, unto the third and to the fourth generation.

And Moses made haste, and bowed his head toward the earth, and worshipped.

And he said If now I have found grace in thy sight, O Lord, let my Lord, I pray thee, go among us; for it is a stiff necked people; and pardon our iniquity and our sin, and take us for your inheritance.

And He said, Behold, I make a covenant: before all thy people I will do marvels, such as have not been done in all the earth, nor in any nation: and all the people of which you are from shall see the work of the Lord: for it is a terrible thing that I will do with you.

Observe you that which I command thee this day: behold, I drive out before thee the Amorite, and the Canaanite, and the Hittite, and the Perizzite, and the Hivite, and the Jebusite.

Take heed to thyself, lest you make a covenant with the inhabitants of the land whither you go, lest it be for a snare in the midst of thee:

But you shall destroy their altars, break their images, and cut down their groves:

For you will worship no other God: for the Lord, whose name is Jealous, is a jealous God:

Lest you make a covenant with the inhabitants of the land, and they go a whoring after their gods, and do sacrifice unto their gods and one call thee, and you eat of his sacrifice;

And you take of their daughters unto thy sons, and their daughters go a whoring after their gods, and make thy sons go a whoring after their gods.

You will make thee no molten gods.

The Feast of Unleavened Bread will you keep. Seven days you will eat unleavened bread, as I commanded thee, in the time of the month Abib: for in the month Abib you came out from Egypt.

All that opens the womb is mine; and every firstling among thy cattle, whether ox or sheep, that is male.

But the firstling of an ass you will redeem with a lamb: and if you redeem him not, then will you break his neck. All the firstborn of thy sons you will redeem. And none shall appear before me empty.

Six days you will work, but on the seventh day you will rest: in seedtime and in harvest you will rest.

And you will observe the feast of weeks, of the first fruits of wheat harvest, and the feast of ingathering at the year's end.

Three times in the year shall all your men appear before the Lord God, the God of Israel.

For I will cast out the nations before thee, and enlarge thy borders: neither shall any man desire thy land, when you will go up to appear before the Lord thy God thrice in the year.

You will not offer the blood of my sacrifice with leaven; neither shall the sacrifice of the feast of the Passover be left unto the morning.

*The first of the first fruits of thy land you will bring unto the
	house of the Lord thy God. You will not seethe a kid in
	his mother's milk.*

*And the Lord said unto Moses, Write you these words: for
	after the tenor of these words I have made a covenant with
	thee and with Israel.*

*And he was there with the Lord forty days and forty nights; he
	did neither eat bread, nor drink water. And he wrote upon
	the tables the words of the covenant, the Ten
	Commandments.*

*And it came to pass, when Moses came down from Mount
	Sinai with the two tables of testimony in Moses' hand,
	when he came down from the mount, that Moses knew not
	that the skin of his face shone while he talked with him.*

*And when Aaron and all the children of Israel saw Moses,
	behold, the skin of his face shone; and they were afraid to
	come nigh him.*

*And Moses called unto them; and Aaron and all the rulers of
	the congregation returned unto him: and Moses talked with
	them.*

*And afterward all the children of Israel came nigh and he gave
	them in commandment all that the Lord had spoken with
	him in Mount Sinai.*

*And till Moses had done speaking with them, he put a veil on
	his face.*

*But when Moses went in before the Lord to speak with him, he
	took the veil off, until he came out. And he came out, and
	spoke unto the children of Israel that which he was
	commanded.*

*And the children of Israel saw the face of Moses, that the skin
	of Moses' face shone: and Moses put the veil upon his face
	again, until he went in to speak with him."*

Jesus finished in the same whisper that he had begun, close to a half-hour later. At the last word, he sat down again as the family members stared in open mouth wonder at the boy who could quote so accurately from the Holy Torah.

Joseph turned to Jesus as the boy landed back down on his seat cushion. "What made you pick that particular passage, Jesus?"

"I remembered that the Passover was mentioned in the middle and thought it might be appropriate," said Jesus.

"It was very appropriate, although I don't think I have ever heard that particular passage of the Law told on a Passover night," said Joseph, who then smiled at his oldest son. "From the looks on their faces, I don't think any of them have either." The rest of the night was spent in remembering the great things God had done and no small amount of questions were tossed at Jesus, Joseph and Mary in relation to the incredible feat the boy had done that night. Many started out by asking how long Jesus had been practicing such a recitation only to be further stunned when he told them that as far as he knew, he had only listened to the passage once, about a year and a half ago.

Sitting with Jesus throughout the night was his cousin John, who along with his mother Elizabeth had come from Jericho earlier in the afternoon. The boys had talked earlier in the day when the mother and son had first gotten there and now the two were inseparable, as were their mothers.

"Why don't you drink any of the wine?" asked Jesus. "I noticed that throughout the whole meal and ceremony you didn't even take a sip."

"My father was instructed by an angel before I was born to raise me as a Nazirite," answered John. "I will never have my hair cut, nor am I allowed to drink anything fermented."

"Wow," said Jesus. "You're a living Nazirite vow. I didn't know people still made those vows any more. Elisha was a Nazirite and so was Samson."

"I think you are destined to be something other than a carpenter," said John, leaning over to whisper in his cousin's ear. "Either a prophet like myself or maybe a Pharisee or a rabbi. I can't see someone with your knowledge of the Scriptures carving wood his whole life."

"You're the one who feels led to be a prophet, not me," said Jesus with a laugh. "I'm just fine with what the Lord has planned for me. You want to go down and swim around in the muddy Jordan River, that's between you and God." The night passed into the bright sunshine of morning and the family broke up to go rest in their respective tents. The day would be spent in slumber as the people prepared for the Sabbath that would come with the setting of the sun.

For many, including the group from Nazareth, the day after the Sabbath would signal the time for the return trip up north. After a full night being awake, many sought to get as much rest as they could get.

The children needed only a few hours before they were fully rested; however they were careful to play and explore away from the camp so as to let their parents, relatives and neighbors sleep.

Thirty-One

Man of Israel

The boy had been enthralled the day his mother and father brought him to the temple. The place felt so right to him, he knew this was where he belonged. He was disturbed by some of the things going on in the courtyard though. He observed blemished animals that were being sold for sacrifice and he knew that God deserved and demanded only the very best according to the Law of Moses. He reasoned that if it was obvious to him, a country boy on his first trip to the temple, than it should have been obvious to the priests and their helpers.

The sellers of these animals were not even servants of the Most High God of creation; they were merchants of all nationalities who had set up their money tables just outside the beautiful gate, in the court of the Gentiles and the look on their faces told the whole story. They were not concerned about worship to God; they were there for the profit and the ritual. The priest and Levites that worked there didn't seem to care about the mockery that was being made in the temple area. Their attitude, thought the boy, was really lousy.

The boy shrugged off the bad thoughts and forgave the ones that were perpetuating this travesty. He figured that they probably didn't know what they were really doing and if they did ever find out, they would probably stop. The boy entertained an idea that maybe he should go tell the chief priest and point out the problems but something told him that now was not the right time; that he would have a chance to do something about it later, he just needed to be patient.

The boy went back to admiring the temple and was caught up in the fact that it was here, and no other place in the whole country, or for that fact, the world, where God had resided. It was right here, on this very mountain, on this very spot, that the glory of the Lord had descended when the people and their king had dedicated another temple, much like this one but even grander, to the God of creation years before.

He had looked up at the Holy Place and in his mind's eye could see through to the back, at the curtain separating the world from the presence of God. That curtain was right where it had always been since the Temple had been rebuilt and when he thought about it he instinctively wanted to go and rip it down. God should not be separated from man. He knew, like no one else there, that God only wanted fellowship with His creation. He shouldn't be kept away in a dark room, lit only by dim candles. The boy felt drawn to the Holy of Holies like a bee to sweet flowers. His parents had introduced him to the chief priest that first day and had gained permission for him to sacrifice with the family and be welcomed in the circle of men.

"Ah yes," said the priest to Jesus and his parents. "You are the lad Rabbi Moshe talked to me about just this morning."

"Yes, sir," said Jesus. "He had said that he was going to talk to you about me."

"Yes, well, he did," said the priest. "It's very unusual for a boy your age to pass into manhood but Moshe said that you were ready. Are you?"

"Sir, I would like to start attending school as soon as I can," said Jesus. "I would also like to take my turn reading from the Torah in our synagogue."

"Then it is granted," said High Priest Mishael. "May I have the yarmulke that you have prepared for your son," he asked Joseph while stretching out his hand toward the carpenter.

"Here it is," said Joseph as he handed the prayer covering to the priest. "May he never find himself without it and be shamed in front of God."

"You are now responsible before God and man to keep the Law that He gave to His servant Moses," intoned the priest as he place the yarmulke on the boy's head. "The sins of your fathers will not be held against you and your sins will not be held against them."

"Before God, I will keep his law," said Jesus. "In my heart, I will hide His words. I will not sin against God or man." He was a man in the eyes of his country's people now. He must take responsibility for himself and represent himself to God. Jesus took this responsibility seriously; he knew he had passed the age of accountability and no one, not even his parents, stood between him and God.

"Father of this new man," said the high priest turning to Joseph. "Let me encourage you to celebrate this occasion with a generous sacrifice of thanksgiving to the Lord. The boy's majority should not go unnoticed by God. You can find sheep and goats over there," motioned the priest, willing them to buy a large and expensive animal to sacrifice.

"The whole family can celebrate at the altar along with the many priests who help with the ritual and gain their sustenance from the daily sacrifices," the priest reminded them. "If you do not have the proper temple coin, the money changers are on the opposite end of the court. Now, if you will excuse me, I must go," said the priest who then walked away.

Joseph and Mary thought over what the priest had suggested and decided to wait. They had planned a party for their oldest son when they got back up north to their own village and were not really prepared to foot the cost of an additional sacrifice, especially one as big as what the priest had recommended. Joseph thought the priest looked a little too big anyway. The man appeared to eat meat every day and probably at every meal. Joseph wondered if the man tried to talk everyone into an extra sacrifice. If he had suggested a grain offering or perhaps a turtledove, Joseph may have gone for it, but a lamb or goat was out of his league.

They just turned to go, after thanking the priest and made their way out of the beautiful gate the way they had come. Joseph gave his son some money to buy a cup full of grain to sacrifice as a peace and thanksgiving offering for all God had done.

After his first Passover meal as a man and his first sacrifice made to Jehovah Himself, the boy was lost in love for the God of the universe. He wanted to know more, he wanted to study, and he wanted to give his life to this most wonderful God. He knew, without having to be told, that he would serve God for the rest of his days.

He knew and understood that he was an apprentice carpenter to his earthly father and that he was expected as the oldest son to follow in his footsteps. Yet at the same time he also realized that study with the local rabbi back in his home could not teach him the things he wanted to know. Many of those things that some of the men walking around the temple had been studying had taken the dedication of their entire lives. He said a prayer there on the spot, asking the Father the answer to his dilemma.

The boy had wandered off to see the splendor of the temple, after giving the priest his cupful of grain, when his parents had called to him and he left to go with them. He wanted to come back tomorrow. He would come back tomorrow. As he was leaving, he spied boys of his age coming away from Solomon's Porch, in the courtyard.

"What are those boys doing over there?" Jesus asked his parents.

"Those boys are a year or more older than you are," said Mary. "They live around here and instead of going to a synagogue to go to school, they attend here."

"When we get back to Nazareth, you will be eligible to study at the synagogue with Rabbi Moshe," said Joseph to the new man of Israel. "Both your grandfather and I studied at that same synagogue, although Rabbi Moshe wasn't the teacher at that time.

"Is Rabbi Moshe as good a teacher as the rabbis they have here?" asked the boy to his parents. He was looking at them with little joy in his face as he contemplated learning from the humorless rabbi whose best skill seemed to be putting little boys to sleep rather than teaching them the law and prophets. "Some of the boys at home complain that the rabbi puts them to sleep when he talks. I even see men and women on the Sabbath nodding off when he is talking."

"The men of the town trust the rabbi," said Joseph who had a look of annoyance for his very perceptive son. "While he is not the best teacher, he is of good moral character." The boy said nothing to this answer, knowing without knowing how he knew; that what man saw to be righteousness was nothing but filthy rags to the Heavenly Father.

Jesus and his parents were walking toward the Straight Gate in the Temple. They were just rounding a corner when they were run into by one of the boys from the school.

"Oh, sorry," said the boy after picking himself up out of the dirt. "I guess I wasn't looking where I was going." He looked at the family with which he had collided. "You're new here," the boy said to Jesus. "I'm Lazarus," he said introducing himself first to Jesus and then to Mary and Joseph.

"I'm Jesus," said the carpenter's apprentice who held out his hand to the other boy. "I'm not from around here. I live in Nazareth in Southern Galilee."

"Oh," said Lazarus. "I'm sorry to crash into you like that. I live about two miles away from here in Bethany and my parents like me to be home before dark."

"No problem," said Joseph. "Just watch the corners next time," he said as he and his wife started on their way again.

"Well, I have to go," said Jesus. "I'll come back tomorrow and maybe we can talk some more."

"Ok," said Lazarus. "I'll look for you tomorrow. Hey, if it's alright with your parents, maybe you can come home with me tomorrow?"

"That would be great," said Jesus who was pleased to have made a new friend so fast. "I'll ask them if I can."

"Ok," said Lazarus, whose eyes then clouded over. "I'll ask my mom if that's all right and let you know tomorrow."

"See ya," said Jesus, who turned and ran after his parents to catch up. "Can I go over to Lazarus's house tomorrow?" asked Jesus as he fell in step with his parents.

"Uh, we'll see if there is time," said Joseph. "We are supposed to leave for home sometime."

Thirty-Two

Return Home

"It was a good time in the city," Joseph mused, as he poked at the fire in front of him. "It was good to be with family and to visit with aunts, uncles, and cousins that we have not seen in the past year."

Passover was always a good time to spend with family and to get a break from his work. With his wife and children along this time for the first time ever, it was a blessed time indeed. As Joseph huddled around the fire to keep warm, he couldn't help but think that life had turned out all right. It had been hard at first, even crazy at times, always moving, never being settled. He and Mary had finally gotten over those early bumps and were now comfortable in the life they had.

Mary had given him wonderful children, the oldest of whom was learning his trade. Joseph admitted to himself that it was nice to have another set of hands around the shop to help him out. His business was picking up and the boy was nicely picking up the slack. At the thought of Jesus, Joseph looked around and wondered where he was. The young man usually stayed closed to his parents and while he was kind of shy and quiet, was growing into a strong and intelligent man. On the way down from Nazareth, he had handled himself like a man, not hiding like a child would, but taking responsibility for his mother, sisters, and brother.

In fact, in the eyes of their faith, he was now a man. Returning from his first trip to the temple, the day after Passover, his oldest son had been confirmed a man among the people and fit to take his place in the religious life of his nation. Rabbi Moshe had really come through and his boy was now no longer a boy. He was now someone who could walk with him to the nightly fires and sit with him in the synagogue. "That will be nice," said Joseph out loud to no one in particular.

Not seeing him, Joseph figured the young man to be with some of the relatives or other town's folk that they were traveling back with on the three-day journey north to where their home was.

"Joseph, there you are," said a rather fat man who Joseph recognized as an uncle from his mother's side of the family. "I need to talk with you."

"Hello uncle …? Hello uncle," said Joseph who could not remember the man's name. "What can I do for you?"

"I had this wheel changed out on my wagon right before I came down from Cana to join the caravan there in Nazareth," said the nameless uncle. "It did fine on the way up to Jerusalem but now it's starting to make a noise."

"What kind of noise?" asked Joseph who really didn't want to do any work while on holiday.

"It's just a funny noise," said the uncle. "Can you look at it?"

"I don't have the tools to do any kind of work," said Joseph, who knew he had enough with him to probably do any kind of job needed for an emergency repair. "When I get home I'll gladly look at it for you, before you head north."

"Well, OK," said the uncle, who really wanted the carpenter to look at it now. "If you think it will wait." Joseph went back to tending the fire without another thought of his oldest son. "I should have gotten some iron nails while in Jerusalem," thought Joseph who then stood up as the fire blazed.

"Mary," Joseph called out. "The fire is ready for cooking."

"Oh, good," said Mary who came over from the family's cart with a pot in her hands. Joseph backed up to let his wife get to the fire and ran into the nameless uncle again.

"If I needed another wheel," asked the uncle. "Would you have one ready to go at your shop?"

"Why don't you just sit down," said Joseph who knew there was no escape. "Just because there is a noise doesn't mean you will need a new wheel," he explained. Joseph looked up from the face of his uncle and saw Mary behind him. She mouthed something to him and Joseph smiled.

"I think, Uncle Zach," Joseph said. "The wheel will be fine. It's probably just wet." His thoughts on Jesus were lost as he tried to reassure the uncle and himself that the wheel would be all right for the next couple of days. The first day after leaving Jerusalem was always a trying one for Mary. There were so many things that could only be bought in Jerusalem that shopping kept her busy for at least a whole day every time she traveled down south. In the city people could worship, every day, if they wanted to, at the Temple

Mary always felt good about going to the Temple. This trip was the first time her oldest son had been able to go into the temple and participate in the religion that so dominated her life. The rules and the law said you had to be thirteen, and he had just turned twelve, but for mature children and those that come from prominent or rich families, the High Priest made exceptions. Only she and Joseph, knew just how exceptional Jesus truly was.

Thoughts of Jesus made Mary swell up with pride. He was such a good boy. There were a few who had made such a big to-do over him when he was born, and Mary had never forgotten the visitation of all those strange shepherds and noblemen, not to mention that other one. Those people who had spoken of many marvelous things had never returned and her son was now growing to be a fine young man and was taking up the family business from his father. Mary kept many secrets in her heart and it was only at times like these that she remembered that her son was destined for something else, or so the angel had told her. Something, she reminded herself, that she didn't understand and was afraid to ask God about.

While she was at the temple, she had wanted to ask a priest or learned doctor of the Law about what had happened twelve years ago. Every time she made up her mind to do so, something happened and she never got around to doing it. Maybe next year, she thought. With both Joseph and Jesus in Jerusalem for Passover now, she would not be long up north before she would get to come again. At least not twelve years, she thought.

Thinking of her son, she wondered where he was. It wasn't like him to not be around. It wasn't like he was loud or obnoxious; he was quite the opposite of that. It was just that he had a presence that you could almost feel. Mary started to leave the midday meal that she was making for her family and relatives that were traveling with her to go look for him, but then reasoned that he was probably with Philip or another of his cousins or friends out playing. Or maybe, she thought, he was with his father, after all, the two now worked together and usually could be found together, just about anywhere either of them went.

She had spied Joseph earlier, talking to an uncle of his about a wagon or something. She had walked over and stood behind the uncle and silently, only moving her lips, reminded Joseph that he was talking to his uncle Zach. She knew her husband tended to be forgetful, especially about people's names. She saw it as one of her wifely duties to help him with it. Seeing his smile and twinkle in his eye that was reserved only for her, she had walked away. She didn't remember seeing Jesus with Joseph then, but he was probably around somewhere, she thought.

With the meal almost ready she would see both husband and son in a little while. With that settled she removed the rock cover of her travel stove and checked the bread to see if it had risen any higher than the last time she had checked. Noticing little black spots starting to form around the bottom edge of the loaf, she quickly removed the rounded snack for her family and busily prepared the rest of the meal, all thoughts of Jesus forgotten.

Thirty-Three

Hellos with No Good-byes

The day dawned bright and already unseasonably warm. Jesus awoke early and ate his breakfast just as soon as his mother could fix it. "I'm going to go back to the Temple and see if Lazarus is there," said Jesus to his mother, who was busy serving the rest of the family.

"Ok," she said smiling at him, not really paying attention. "Don't be gone long."

"I won't be," said the boy half hearing his mother's reply as he hurriedly walked away from the camp. Jesus made his way back to the Temple and as if by design ran into Lazarus, literally, as he turned the corner of the main building. Laughing as they picked themselves up, as they had done the day before, the two were fast friends by the time they got to their feet.

"Don't you ever slow down going around corners?" asked Jesus. "One of these days you're going to run into one of the fat priests and die."

"I never do anything slow," said Lazarus. "I talked to my mom and she said that you could come home tonight for supper."

"Great," said Jesus. "Is Bethany a large town?"

"Naw," said Lazarus. "We just have a couple of hundred people."

"Wow," said Jesus. "Nazareth is bigger than that"

"By the way," said Lazarus who just remembered what else his mother had told him. "My mom said that you can come over but you can't bother my two sisters. They're learning how to clean and cook and she doesn't want them side-tracked."

"I have sisters of my own," said Jesus. "The last thing I want is to hang around them."

"Yeah," said Lazarus in agreement. "They're a pain anyway. The farther we are away from them the better." At about that time he was finishing his speech about his sisters, a pious looking man who obviously thought himself very important put a ram's horn to his lips and blew a quick five snorts.

"I gotta go to school," said Lazarus. "That was the sound of doom. What are you doing right now?"

"Nothing," said Jesus who hadn't thought about what he would do while waiting for his new friend. "Can I sit in on your class? Do you think your rabbi would mind?"

"You want to come to class?" asked the stunned boy who gave him a sideways look that conveyed just how crazy he thought Jesus to be and just shook his head. "School is a drag. Nobody likes going. All they teach you is stuff about dead people and then they have you read more stuff written by dead people about the other dead people. If I were you I would go to the market place,"

Jesus had so many questions for Lazarus at that point that he nearly burst. How could anyone be bored with the things of God? How could it be a drag? The God he knew was definitely not a drag, every day was exciting and new with the God he worshipped – the very God of this temple.

"I'll go, if it's all right," said Jesus. "I'll take my chances. No one could be more boring than my rabbi at home."

"All right, but you'll be sorry," said Lazarus, shaking his head like he was being slapped silly by two hands one right after the other. "The torture pit is right this way." The rabbi stopped Jesus before he went into the classroom situated in a building beside the main temple. After ascertaining that the boy was visiting from up north and that he was a guest of Lazarus, the rabbi allowed him to sit beside Lazarus on the floor in front of the raised platform that was soon occupied by the teaching rabbi of the day.

The lesson for the day for the boys of Lazarus's age was out of the Law. The rabbi wanted the boys to discuss the merits of Noah and his family and why exactly did God allow them to live while the rest of the world had to die. The discussion was in full swing when Jesus piped in.

"Noah's family deserved the same fate as the rest of the world," he said. "It was only because God knew that Noah would not want to see his family destroyed that God allowed them to live." This comment grabbed the attention of the rabbi who had been helping the older boys who were involved in a heated debate over the meaning of the bones in Ezekiel. He wandered over to the younger group just as Jesus had finished his speech about Noah.

"Why don't you think the family of Noah was not pleasing to God," asked the rabbi.

"Well, sir," answered Jesus. "No one is pleasing to a Holy God except for those who approach Him by faith. The Torah points out that Noah is the only human being that found grace in the sight of the Lord at that time."

"I see," said the rabbi nodding to the young man in front of him. "Who is your rabbi up north?"

"I just got confirmed at the temple," said Jesus. "When I go home I will sit under Rabbi Moshe."

"Really?" said the rabbi who seemed troubled at the answer. "So where did you learn about the Law of Moses. Is your father a Pharisee? Whose opinion is this that you are telling?" Surely, he was thinking, the boy had to have picked up that doctrine from someone. After all, there were no noted rabbis or teachers in Nazareth. Really, he thought, those second class Jews were really not noted for anything, except of course, for being way up north with the hated Samaritans in between.

Before he could really inquire into specifics with the boy, the horn blew again and the class was over. Jesus got up with Lazarus who was already making his way to the door and freedom.

"Sir, could I come back tomorrow?" asked Jesus. "I'll try and answer your questions then."

"Of course," said the curious rabbi. "Peace be with you."

"Peace be with you too, revered teacher," said Jesus with the formal reply. The rabbi wanted to talk with this boy some more, he thought, as he made his way to the rack of scrolls to read again the account of the flood. The teacher was considered an expert on the Law, especially from creation to Abraham, and was frequently consulted by the high priest and the chief teachers at the temple. He had never heard the theory put forth by the boy and he thought he had read through and had listened to all the commentaries from rabbis from as far back as the time of Joshua.

As he read, he began to see how the boy was right. Young Jesus had quoted the scripture accurately and had lain open an entirely new way of interpreting that portion of the Law. As the hours passed into the night, the rabbi studied as if drinking water after a long trip through the Negev. He had commented on the text he was reading to several rabbis and priests that had come in looking for him and they had promised to come back to see the boy the next day.

They were anxious to learn whom the teacher up north was who had brought a new light to the scriptures that they held so dear. They had asked about his parents, if anything was known about them. Children, up until the time that they were sent to the Pharisees at the local synagogue, were supposed to be taught by their parents. They were to do nothing formal, just cover all the major historical stories. To teach your child a new doctrine apart from the Pharisees was not normal and could potentially be extremely dangerous.

The teacher yawned then, noticing that the sun had gone down. He was not used to staying at the porch beside the temple for so long; being at times just as anxious as his charges about leaving after the lessons for the day was over. He was hungry also, which was a rarity. Usually he was home. His normal lifestyle dictated that he had regular meal times; and as for creature comforts, he lacked for little.

If the truth were told, he had not been this driven to study for quite some time. He definitely would talk with the boy tomorrow and get to the bottom of this controversy. He could handle it, he thought, no reason to get the chief priest involved yet, but he did want to see if there was any other strange teaching going on up north.

Heresy was a serious matter, and even though the boy was right about Noah and his family, it was a new teaching, and to his and his colleagues' minds, that was bad. It was their responsibility to watch over the Law and preserve it intact for the generations to come. It was rumored that the Messiah would soon appear and they would not like to be caught as false teachers by Him.

Thirty-Four

Friends for Life

With Lazarus leading the way after school, both boys made their way to the eastern part of the Temple, down the stairs and out the east gate, also called the Golden Gate, which was an exit of the city.

Halfway across the bridge that spanned the Cedron Brook, Jesus stopped short. "Oh, oh," said Jesus. "I need to go back to the camp and tell my parents where I'm going. They tend to get worried over nothing sometimes."

"Ok," said Lazarus. "We need to hurry though. Mom is going to have supper prepared and I'm really hungry." They ran up the hill and back into the temple, climbing the stairs and turning immediately to the right and walking straight through the sheep gate at the northern end of the temple grounds. After rounding Antonia Tower, with its massive bulwarks and fortifications, they angled left and headed, as straight as they could to the Fish Gate that would let them outside the city on the north side.

Jesus thought as they walked through the gate that these were the same walls that Jeremiah had built along with the people he had brought back from Babylon. Jesus could just see the men, women and children working on the wall, transporting rock in one hand while brandishing a sword with the other, just in case the wicked Sanballet and his gang of thugs should come along.

After a 15-minute walk, the two boys came to the pilgrim campgrounds that were located under the shadow of the walls. Jesus was stunned to behold an empty lot. "Every body's gone!" exclaimed Jesus in shock. The ground was well policed, the privacy holes filled in and the animal pens and tents taken up as though no one was never there. "Dad said that they might be leaving sometime. How could they forget me?"

In the rush of packing the caravan for the three-day trip home, his parents must just have assumed that he was in the company somewhere. Packing was always a busy time and the children were either put to work or sent away rather than have them under foot.

"I guess I should go after them," said Jesus to his amused friend. "They can't be that far up the road."

"Do you know what time they left?" asked Lazarus who walked toward one of the campfire cooking rings. "The fires aren't even smoldering," he said as he reached down to touch the ashes.

"I haven't a clue," said Jesus watching his friend. "I was with you all day."

"Well, it's been hours," said Lazarus standing up from the fire ring. "You would have to travel all night just to catch up. Do you know what route they took?"

"No," said Jesus. "Is there more than one?"

"Come on," said Lazarus shaking his head. "You may know about Noah, but you don't know anything about traveling. There is no sense tempting God."

"I would never do that," said Jesus whose head snapped up at the mention of his heavenly father's name. "Should I wait until morning?"

"The road isn't safe for one person to travel alone," said Lazarus. "Better if you just come with me and wait for your parents to come back. You told them whom you were going to be with, didn't you?"

"Yeah, I told my mom this morning," said Jesus. "Okay, let's go, I'm getting hungry." The boys made their way back the way they had come, stopping only once along the way at the pool of Bethesda to get a drink of water. While there, Jesus struck a conversation with a man who had been lame for most of his life.

"You know, an angel of God comes around this pool and stirs the water sometimes," the man said to Jesus and Lazarus. "The first person who can get into the water gets healed. I've seen it myself time and time again."

"Why haven't you gotten in the pool then?" asked Lazarus.

"I'm never close enough to the water when it happens," replied the man bitterly. "And, even if I were, I have no one to put me in it."

"Well," said Lazarus who had no pat answers to give the man. "I hope everything turns out all right for you."

"Maybe God has a different plan for your healing." Jesus said as he turned to follow Lazarus. "Maybe that's why you can never get into the water in time." The man just sighed at the thought and began to complain some more as the boys walked off.

They went out once more through the east gate of the temple, across the bridge and then left down the mountain road to Bethany, the spires and columns of the temple fading away behind them. Jesus was sure as he walked down the road, that he would travel it many times in the years to come. The road wound down to the bottom, where it flattened and straightened out some, going directly for a group of houses that could just be seen in the distance.

"I'll race you to the bottom of the hill?" said Lazarus.

"You're on," said Jesus. Lazarus finished well ahead of Jesus as both boys crossed the finish line huffing and puffing.

"I would have beaten you if I didn't get a rock in my sandal," said Jesus who was limping as he crossed behind the bigger and older boy. "Plus you have the home advantage."

"I've never lost a race yet," said Lazarus. "Next time I'll give you a head start. If you think you need one?"

"There's always a first to everything," said Jesus as the boys walked into the town. "Your first loss will be our next race and no, I won't need a head start to do it. By the way," Jesus said, before Lazarus could make another claim. "Is there anything I should know before I get to your house? I mean, I am going to be spending the night. I don't want to break any rules or anything."

"Just stay away from my sisters and you'll be fine," said Lazarus. "We'll hit up my mom first thing and tell her what's happened."

"So what are their names?" asked Jesus.

"The oldest one is Martha and the younger one is Mary," answered Lazarus.

"Mary is a pretty common name," Jesus said. "My mother is also named Mary.

"Yeah, I guess it is," said Lazarus. "I had an uncle that was named Lazarus. I was named after him.

"Really?" said Jesus. "You're the first Lazarus that I've ever met."

"Well, I hope I don't end up like him," said Lazarus. "He died before I was born. I guess he fell on hard times and became a beggar to the rich man who bought his land. The rich man didn't observe the ancient rules of mercy. My uncle starved to death right outside the door of that rich man. I wonder if God will punish that rich man? Apparently they died around the same time."

"For sure your uncle is safely in the bosom of Abraham awaiting the end of the age," Jesus told his friend. "I doubt the rich man is in any comfort at all about this time."

"So, are you ready for another race," asked Lazarus. "That's my house right over there," he said pointing up the road. By way of answer to the challenge, Jesus just took off, with Lazarus trailing behind. Without the rock in his sandal, Jesus was standing around the house with a bored expression on his face, as if he had been waiting for a long time, when Lazarus, huffing and puffing, finally came to a halt.

"I think that makes us even," said Jesus with a curious expression on his face. "I hope the feeling of losing doesn't kill you."

"Whatever," said Lazarus who was not used to losing. "We'll run again tomorrow. All the extra walking you had me do tired me out more than I thought."

"Whenever and wherever is fine with me," said Jesus. "So this is your house?"

"Yeah," said Lazarus who entered the two-story, horseshoe shaped home with Jesus right behind him. "Mom, I'm home and I brought Jesus with me," shouted the boy. Lazarus's mother was in the upper part of the house and could be heard coming down the stairs that had been built toward the back of the open room.

"How was your day at the Temple?" asked the boy's mother, who stopped in front of her son and extended her cheek.

"Fine," said Lazarus who, while turning red in the face, bent forward and kissed his mother. "Same as always. This is Jesus."

"Be welcome in our home," said the mother to her guest.

"Peace be unto you and all that live in this house," replied Jesus.

"Can he stay the night?" asked Lazarus. "You won't believe what happened." Lazarus then related the story of the day, how Jesus had come to school with him that morning and had been left behind by his parents. Lazarus' mother just shook her head when she heard the whole story.

"Well," she said. "You're certainly welcome to stay with us for as long as it takes your mother and father to discover you're gone."

"Thank you," said Jesus. "I'm sure it will only be a day or two at the most."

After a quick snack of dried figs and honey, Lazarus's mother told him his father needed him in the fields. The boys had taken their snacks up to the roof patio so as not to be in the way and for some privacy while they talked.

"I'll be back after dark," said the boy with a look that told a story of misery and woe.

"Can I help?" asked Jesus who really didn't want to be left alone in the strange house.

"Why should we both be bummed out," said Lazarus. "Just hang out up here until I get back." Only later, after a good deal of self-pity, did it occur to Lazarus that it was almost dark by the time he left the house. To Lazarus, complaining was an art form that truly intrigued Jesus. Jesus stayed on the roof as the sun set. He liked watching the sun go down. He wondered how far his parents had gone that day and if they had discovered that he was missing. They would never think to look for him here in Bethany, Jesus thought, even though he had told his mom.

He decided he would tell the teacher at the school tomorrow that he was staying with Lazarus, in case his parents came to the temple to look for him. They would know to come to the temple right away, he figured. They must know how much he liked being there. For tonight he would enjoy being away from his parents. He was a man now; anyway, it was only proper to be away from them, if only for a little bit.

The giggling of two raven-headed girls, the oldest of whom looked no more than 10 years old, interrupted his thoughts. Martha, the oldest, looked at Jesus with what could only be construed as a motherly look. Jesus felt the need to go wash in the nearby stream or river in response to the look she gave him. As he looked down on himself, he realized that he was dirty from head to toe.

"You can wash your hands in the bowl of water just inside the main room," said Martha. "Or you can just go to the river and get clean."

"The, ah, bowl should do just fine," said Jesus. "Thank you."

"Make sure you take your sandals off before you come inside too," she said, continuing as though Jesus hadn't said a word. "Lazarus always forgets to do that. Now that I'm in charge of cleaning this house, he's going to remember."

"I'll remember," said Jesus, trying to be friendly with the stern little girl. "We have the same rule at our house.

"Don't make me remind you," Martha said as she squinted her eyes at him. "Visitor or no visitor, my house will stay clean." An uncomfortable silence reigned among the three as they looked back and forth from each other. Jesus didn't say another word; he figured he couldn't have if he wanted to anyway. One thing was for sure, he knew who the boss was. Lazarus had warned him about staying away from his sisters and now he knew why. The silence was broken when the younger of the two, Mary, came forward and bowed low.

"Be welcome in our house," said Mary with a big smile. "Be at ease and feel safe."

"And peace be unto you, little sister," said Jesus returning her smile.

"Oh come on Mary," said Martha as she rolled her eyes at the display. "Mom needs help in the kitchen."

Without so much as a goodbye, she whirled around and turned to go just as Lazarus was coming up the stairs. Martha sat down hard as her forehead stopped abruptly in the chest of Lazarus, who, with three years and 50 pounds on her, towered over his younger sister. Jesus couldn't help the laugh that came boiling up out of him at the site of the imperious Martha sprawled on the floor of the roof, rubbing her forehead that had played tag with the breastbone of Lazarus. He knew full well the feeling of hitting the ground after running into the farmer's son as he had done it twice in the past two days.

Martha, while shooting killing looks at her brother and his friend, gathered herself up, took Mary by the hand, who by now was laughing and giggling along with Jesus, and pounded down the stairs, almost trying, it seemed, to break the boards in two. Lazarus acted like nothing had happened.

"Supper is just about ready," Lazarus said to Jesus. "What's so funny?"

"Nothing, nothing," said Jesus. "So what did your father want you for? It didn't take all that long."

"Oh, that," said Lazarus, who made a face and rolled his eyes in exactly the same way Martha did. "He just wanted some help bringing in some tools from the field." Lazarus turned to go down the stairs that Martha had just tried to destroy with her stomping, and Jesus followed him. Jesus remembered to stop and take off his sandals before he entered the house and even pulled Lazarus back to wash his hands before they entered the main living room. In that room there was a low table with cushions around it that beckoned them to supper. The number one conversational topic that evening over supper was how Jesus' parents could just leave him. Lazarus' father came to their defense.

"What's the biggest trip we make?" asked the father. "Jericho? We don't have the slightest idea what it takes to travel for three days in a caravan with more than 200 people. I don't see how anyone could keep track of anything."

The meal, consisting of roasted lamb and leeks, was simple yet hot and filling. Jesus seemed to be constantly hungry and because he was a growing boy ate more than his fair share. The thought of food was constantly on his mind; it was only when his attention was wholly directed at something else did he not think about feeding his belly. Eating probably more than he should have; his mother despaired of breaking his habit of going back for thirds. He thanked his hosts for their kind hospitality, directing even a kind smile to Martha, who, in turn, gave him a suspicious look.

Mary, who had been the first to finish her meal, was at her father's feet, massaging them and listening to him while he talked. She seemed comfortable doing this and did not look in the least bit shy about showing her love toward her father.

"Father," said Martha, who had seen this display before. "Tell Mary to get up and help me with these dishes. With guests here tonight, there are twice as many as usual," exaggerated the workaholic little girl.

"Oh Martha," said the father. "We only had one guest tonight and Jesus used the same plate for all four helpings."

"Why do I have to do all the work?" Martha said, not willing to let her sister get away. "She never does anything."

"Okay, Okay," he said, after receiving a pointed look from his wife who seemed to have the same outlook on priorities as Martha did. "Mary, thank you. You had better get up and go help your sister."

"Yes father," said Mary, who then stuck her tongue out at Martha before she got up to start clearing off plates. As the women cleaned off the remainder of supper from the low table, Lazarus took Jesus into one of the wings of the house, which opened off the main room.

"This is where my sisters and I sleep," said Lazarus. "You can sleep over there in the corner," he said, indicating with his hand the corner that was opposite the place the girls slept."

"Sorry we have to be in the same room with my sisters," Lazarus apologized. "One day, father and I will build on to this house."

"No problem," said Jesus. "I'm used to it, with all the brothers and sisters I have."

"So do you guys have a council fire at night where you come from?" asked Lazarus.

"Yeah," said Jesus. "My father goes every evening. Why?"

"You're a man of Israel now," stated Lazarus. "And a guest. You are expected to go with my father and me tonight. The men and elders like to hear about what's going on outside of Bethany."

"Oh," said Jesus. "I didn't think about that."

"It's torture for me," said Lazarus. "The school age boys get questioned by their fathers and then we have to recite a proverb. I always have trouble thinking up one." Lazarus changed into a fresh cloak and even lent Jesus a clean one to replace the dirt drenched one he had on. When they both finished changing they hurried to the main room in time to see Lazarus's father, with a fresh cloak on himself, adjust his yarmulke on his head and look toward the boys with a smile. Lazarus and Jesus instinctively reached up to their head to make sure their own religious head pieces, resting at the back top of their heads, were in place. To go to the meeting without your head covered was to bring disgrace to your family and neither boy wanted that.

Jesus felt sad. He should have gone to his first men's gathering with his father Joseph. But that was not to be. He briefly wondered if they had discovered him missing yet. He wondered if even now they were in the big city looking for him. Lazarus's father started down the stairs to the first level and Jesus pulled his thoughts back to the present. He would be reunited with his parents, he was sure. In the mean time, he planned on experiencing everything he could; the town that he came from was kind of boring and being this close to the city was very exciting; there was so much to do, especially at the temple. With that thought, he marched down the stairs and out into the night behind Lazarus and his father. He could see the bonfire by the village gates and knew, from his own town that was were the meeting would be held.

Thirty-Five

In Need of Help

Sweat was running down Joseph's face like water leaking from a freshly drawn well bucket that had sprung more than one hole. Uncle Zach's wagon had broken down right after the caravan had stopped for the night. And of course they had just assumed that Joseph, being a carpenter, would fix it. Joseph resigned himself to the fact that there would be no payment for service in this case and that it was he who would not look at the wagon earlier in the day. The fault was his so now the responsibility was also his. The one thing he was stressing to his oldest son about being in business was being responsible and having integrity, even if the person was not dealing the same with you. Sometimes, Joseph thought, dealing with family members was like dealing with tax collectors. A person could never win and therefore, should never try. The hardest and most difficult part of the job was coming up and he needed some help.

"Mary," called Joseph, who caught her eye and waved her over. "Go find Jesus. Tell him I'm gong to need him to put this wheel back on." Joseph took a break, and went to the well they were camping by that night to get a drink of water. The wheel that he had been working on had lost several spokes and had become lopsided. In order to fix it he had had to take it off the wagon with the help of his uncle and cousins. The wheel was now round and true and ready to be mounted back on the wagon, but his former helpers where now nowhere to be found. He wondered, as he walked back up to the wheel and the wagon, what was taking Mary so long in bringing his boy to him. It was only at times like these, when his mind settled on his oldest son that he would remember that he was the boy's stepfather, not his natural father. Joseph had resolved never to tell anyone that Mary had become pregnant before they had been married and that the father had not been him.

If not for the strange man who had visited him in a dream, and told him that God had sent him Himself, Joseph had planned to just walk away from the whole matter and break their engagement. In order to do that by the law, he would have had to expose Mary as pregnant and claim that the child she was with was not his. If he had done that, the people of the town at the very least would have sent her away in shame. The maximum punishment would have seen the whole town come together to stone her. It would have been his "privilege" to cast the first stone.

The strange man, he must have been an angel, for he was easily 10 feet tall, not to mention the six feathered wings that acted like a covering around his midsection; told him to stick with Mary and take her for his wife, and so, Joseph did just that. He loved his wife; he could not bear to think of harm coming to her. He kept his peace all those many years ago and married her. The child he claimed as his own. It was hard to believe that it had been twelve years since all of that had taken place. So much had taken place over the course of those years – the birth of the rest of his children, the trip to Egypt – so much.

Not a soul had he ever told about that angelic visit in his dreams, except for Mary, of course, and she would never tell anyone else. Mary had told him once who the father was. It was hard to believe, but after what had happened to him with the dream and all, Joseph knew it had to be true and put all his faith in the God who he served. After coming back from the foreign nation where they had lived for a few years, after responding to another crazy dream that seemed so real that he had fled with his family that night, Joseph and Mary had settled into a routine life. For some reason Joseph had had a feeling, ever since Mary had told him the origins of the boy, that the boy's father would come calling one day and that Joseph and Mary both would have to let go. Joseph didn't think about it all that much any more, the boy was his responsibility. He would do the best job of parenting he could do and that would have to be good enough.

Joseph's train of thought was broken as Mary came at him running with a panicked look on her face. Joseph noticed that the boy was not with her.

"Oh for heavens sake," said Joseph out loud as Mary got closer. "I need him now. Go back and tell him now!"

"I can't find him," said Mary who was clearly worried. "I can't find him anywhere." Joseph and Mary questioned all the relatives that they'd been traveling with but no one knew where he was. The strange thing was that no one could remember the last time they had seen him. Joseph questioned his other children and the myriad nieces and nephews that his oldest son ran and played with, but to no avail. They had been so busy playing that they had not noticed he was not there. The truth, obvious and terrifying came crashing down on both of them at the same time. Their boy had never left the city with their caravan.

Fear and despair rushed in along with this realization. The city was not a place for a country boy who was alone and apart from his parents for the first time. Where would he stay? What would he eat? They knew for sure that he had little or no money and, being in the city for the first time, would know no one. Jesus would not know to go down to Bethlehem to Mary's relatives, because, except for when he was a baby had never been there and did not know the way.

"I should have checked," said Joseph who was angry with himself. "It's not your fault. The boy is my apprentice, he's usually with me."

"I just thought he was out playing with the other children," said Mary. "When he didn't come to get anything to eat at midday I thought he was with someone else."

"I was thinking about him earlier, at midday," admitted Joseph. "I should have checked then." Joseph could have kicked himself and with great effort, calmed himself as he felt his heart start to pound in his chest.

"He's not here, in the caravan," said Joseph finally. "He must be back in Jerusalem."

"It's not safe there," said Mary on the verge of panic. "We have to go back." Hurriedly, with a great fear and trepidation, Joseph and Mary saddled the swiftest donkey that the family possessed.

"You can stay at the house until we come back," said Joseph to Zebudee and his wife who had volunteered to take care of the other children. "Are you sure your business can wait?"

"You saved my daughter's life, Joseph," said the big fisherman. "The fish will still be there when I get home."

"Thank you my friend," said Joseph.

Joshua was next in line as he stepped forward with both of his sons. "Go with God, Joseph and Mary," said the old tailor as both his sons nodded their heads. "As the Lord returned my son, so He will help you to find yours."

"Thank you Joshua," said Joseph and Mary together.

"I can't go back with you," Joshua said. "So here is some money. You will need speed if you are to get to Jerusalem fast. Use this to stay in a tavern."

As the night finally went from twilight to darkness, they set off for Jerusalem to look for their oldest son. As they went along, both started to pray for the safety and quick reunion with their son.

Thirty-Six

Bonfire Stories

As Lazarus, his father and Jesus arrived at the fire that evening, they could see that there was already a gathering of about 20 men and some 15 boys, some not looking any older than Jesus, who was, he figured, the youngest one there. From what Lazarus had explained to Jesus while on their way to the fire about who sat where and so forth, the young man from Nazareth learned that the oldest men of the town, the elders, usually sat closest to the fire. They were usually positioned upwind of any smoke that the cool evening breeze would push in various directions depending on the season.

Men that were in their prime and had come to realize their full strength of manhood would sit across from the elders and endure the smoke while gleaning wisdom and knowledge from those who had sat where they had been for many years. The places of honor, set aside for guest, traveling priest, Levites or other distinguished visitors to the town, sat close to the fire in-between the elders and men.

Circling the entire group would be the young men, who would have to stand and be ready to answer any of the men who would call on them for an accounting or to run some errand. Because it was disrespectful to stand behind the elders and because the boys did not want smoke in their eyes, the boys could usually be found in between, behind the places of honor. While the places of honor were generally vacant from night to night, tonight's fire revealed that the town of Bethany was hosting a man who looked beat up and bone tired from traveling on the road. Indeed, as Jesus drew closer to the fire and looked across from where he and Lazarus had decided to stand, Jesus noticed that the man still bore a head bandage and that his arm was still in a sling.

The oldest of the elders, Joash, noticed that Jesus was also a stranger among them and rose from his accustomed place to greet the guest of Matthew, Lazarus' father.

"Are you a relative of the family of Matthew?" asked Joash, after he had welcomed Jesus in the traditional way of wishing peace to the one he was addressing.

"Peace to you, eldest father," answered Jesus, who had learned the traditional answer to the greeting while he was still learning how to talk. "I'm a friend of Lazarus, and his parents have asked me to spend the night with them," said Jesus.

"How old are you boy?" asked Joash, who, to his eyes saw a child before him that could have only just recently stopped sucking at his mother's teat.

"I am twelve years old sir," answered Jesus.

"How is it, young man that you wear the yarmulke of a Jewish man of Israel?" Joash inquired. "And, what are you doing here at the congregation of men?"

"The High Priest proclaimed me a man of Israel just a couple of days ago, before the Passover Celebration," answered Jesus. "I received my head covering then. Tonight is my first counsel of men, even though I am far from my home in Nazareth."

Joash smiled at the boy while thinking that he was getting too old. Thinking to make up for the challenge to the boy's right to be there, Joash took Jesus by the arm and led him to the place of honor, opposite the injured stranger.

"Sit down here tonight," said the old man in a conciliatory tone. "You will be a guest of Bethany for your first council fire." The evening started with introductions of the guest and then to news of what was happening in the wide world. The guests were questioned on road conditions and the presence of Roman Legionnaires who normally patrolled the roads and made travel safe.

"My family and I had to fight off a band of thieves on our way up to Jerusalem," said Jesus. "Our caravan was jumped in the mountains of Samaria. We didn't see one soldier on the road the whole time." This information brought cries of anger from the group, especially the older men, who claimed that when they were younger, the roads were safer and the Samaritan roving gangs were dealt with swiftly. They also claimed that they didn't need the Roman soldiers for protection in their day because the Jews themselves would patrol the highways and rain punishment on any that would break the peace.

The men who sat opposite the elders listened patiently for the diatribe to end. This was normal, they thought, for the old men to think things had been better in their day when, in actuality, there was probably less crime on the roads these days than every before. A man thought twice now if he embarked on a life of crime, especially if that profession could get him tied or nailed to a Roman cross for all to see. The stranger, who during introductions, said his name was Micah, waited for the conversation to die down and then gave his story of how he came to be injured and the reason for it. He also alluded to the fact that his story had to do with Samaritans also.

"I was going from Jerusalem to Jericho through the mountain pass a few weeks back, hoping to close a business deal with a fellow merchant that I often do business with," began Micah. "I was on the road at a point where the Gishon River makes a big bend to go around the Mount of Olives on its eastern face when I was jumped and robbed by five or six thieves. Not only did they rob me of the money that I had brought along to consummate the business deal but they also stole my donkey and beat me until I thought for sure that I would die. You can all see the scars that I bear from the ordeal. Indeed, I am still healing and give thanks to God that I can still draw breath to tell this tale. The men left me for dead, knowing that if I didn't expire soon from my wounds, that I would be attacked and carried off for food by some beast that prowls at night. I laid there, beside the road knowing that soon I would be dead and my family would fall on hard times.

It was perhaps about an hour after the robbers had left when I heard a donkey coming from the direction of Jericho. I lifted my head and saw a man dressed as a priest making his way to the Temple in Jerusalem. I cried out to the priest to have mercy on me and to help me. He slowed down and bent his head to look upon me, but seeing the dire condition I was in, passed me by, not saying a word. The priest didn't even offer me a prayer", told Micah.

At this, the men of the town of Bethany grumbled and muttered in agreement with each other that good priests were nowhere to be found and that most of them were no better than the thieves who preyed on innocent travelers like Micah. After cursing the heartless priest, the men quieted down once more to listen to more of the traveler's story.

Jesus, for his part, was close to tears. He knew that priests were supposed to represent the best of God and were to be His ambassadors to the people of Israel. For one to show no pity and to pass by without stopping for one, who was in such dire need, was a sad testimony to the priesthood in general. Jesus thought once more on his thoughts that maybe things were much more corrupt at the temple than even anyone realized. Micah interrupted his thoughts and lamenting when the forsaken traveler continued his story.

"There I laid, tears in my eyes and fury building up inside of me. I could see that it was only a few more hours until night fell and all I could do was drag myself until I was on the side of the road. I don't remember much after that because I was racked in a mighty pain and passed out for while. When I came to I saw a man walking up the road in the same direction that the priest had been going. I called to him for help when he drew near, although my voice was but a croaking noise that even I could not recognize as coming from me. I could tell from the robe he was wearing that he was a Levite, one who serves the holy places, in the Temple and other locations around Israel," said Micah.

The men around the fire were intent on the stranger's story, and unlike other nights, even the boys and young men gave their full attention to him. Jesus listened, almost not breathing as he stared at the man. He was thinking and hoping, like the others, that the Levite would have surely stopped and helped the dying man.

"The Levite did not stop for me," said Micah, as if reading the minds of his listeners. "He would not even look me in the eye as he passed, he didn't even slow his pace." The men around the bonfire shook their heads in disbelief, but unlike before made no comments or curses. They all privately wondered what their country was coming to that no one would stop to help what was clearly a helpless and wounded countryman on a dangerous road. Every one around the fire leaned forward and waited as the stranger collected himself from the trauma of the memory. A few moments later, he continued.

"I knew I was done for then, for I could see the shadows growing longer and I began to wish that I would just die then, for I did not want to die a horrible death at the claws and teeth of some wild beast. I blacked out again, the pain being too much, although I suspect that I had also lost too much blood.

I awoke, it seems, in the dark, although, when I fully came out of my stupor, I realized that it was twilight and that while the sun could not be seen, having gone down behind the mountain that towered above me, it was yet not dark. A man was binding up my broken arm and had wrapped some sort of cloth around my head. When he stood up to return to his donkey, I could see that he had torn his own cloak to attend to my wounds. He led his donkey over to where I lay and then stood over me, looking at me with an appraising look in his eye. I knew not what he was thinking, but thought that he was giving me one last glance before he too went his own way, having preserved me only for the animals to get at later that night.

Then he bent down and with a grunt that belied the fact that I had eaten too well for too long, he hefted me up and put me upon his donkey, laying me across the animal's back. With that, he took the beast's reins and started walking, toward Jericho."

Micah stopped to take a drink of strong wine that was offered to him by unseen hands that offered the skin over his right shoulder. He took the skin in his left hand; his right still bound in the sling, and tilted it up. The young man that stood behind him dutifully squeezed the skin that would allow the wine to pour in the thirsty stranger's mouth. With a word of thanks, Micah wiped his mouth and prepared to finish his story.

"It was very dark and late when we stopped at the Roman way inn in the town of Anathoth, which is half-way between Jerusalem and Jericho. The man took me down off the donkey and inquiring as to how I felt, left me propped up against the side of the inn wall and went inside to wake the manager of the roadside inn. The man had said little to me on the road, and if the truth were known, I was in no condition to talk. While the donkey was better than walking, it was still a bumpy ride and my wounds hurt.

The man came back out and helped me inside the inn where he took me to a room and laid me down on a well-appointed pallet, filled with feathers and covered in linen. I could hear the man say more words to the innkeeper and then no more as I once more passed out. I woke the next morning and discovered that my head and arm had been freshly bandaged. I could also feel bandages that wrapped up both my knees. They were scraped, I guess, when I dragged myself up from the ditch where the robbers had thrown me. The innkeeper came in then and introduced himself to me as Lukas. He was a Greek, and tended the inn for the Romans.

I asked him if he thought I would die and he said that with care, I would mend. I told him about my being robbed and informed him that I could not pay him right away for his services. Lukas looked at me and smiled and said that the man who had brought me in had already paid in advance for my care. This innkeeper told me that the man had left instructions that if the payment wasn't enough, that when he came back by the next time he was going that way, he would settle up then.

I was amazed, for I didn't even know the name of the man who saved me. I inquired if the man was still at the inn, but Lukas informed me that the strange man had left at first light to continue his journey, back on the road. I asked if the man had left his name, but Lukas shook his head."

"He comes by maybe twice a year. He spends the night and leaves. Always pays in advance and is gone with the first rising of the sun," said Lukas.

"I asked if he knew anything else about the man, what kind of business he was in or where he came from. The only answer that Lukas could give me was that the man was not a Jew like me. Micah looked around at the faces that stared intently at him. He knew that what he would tell them next would forever change the thinking of each of these men and boys. With a deep breath, he finished his story. "The man who helped me was a Samaritan," exclaimed Micah. It was at this statement that everyone it seemed spoke at once.

The fire counsel ended without the usual proverb sparring that was enjoyed and practiced for during the day. The revelation of Micah about the identity of his savior coupled with the troubling behavior of those who had refused to help him had given everyone present much to think about. Jesus had thanked everyone who came to shake his hand for the hospitality shown to him and then left with Matthew and Lazarus, as they made their way back to their home.

"I don't care what that traveler said tonight," Matthew told the boys as they walked. "There may be one decent Samaritan out there somewhere, but I haven't seen him yet and until I do, I'll despise them to my dying breath."

"But father, don't they believe in the same God we do?" asked Lazarus.

"Not really," said Matthew, who then went on to explain. "In the beginning, when Israel was united under Kings David and Solomon, we all worshipped the same God at the Temple in Jerusalem. When the kingdoms split, the upper or northern 10 tribes fell away into idolatry. They tried to build their own temple to God at Samaria so those people wouldn't need to come to Jerusalem ever year. The wicked kings that led them elevated their own priest and instituted their own traditions in their made up, false temple. In short, they led the people astray from what were the commandments of God," said Matthew as the threesome approached the farmer's family house.

"Sit on the steps, you two, and I will finish the story," said Matthew, who thought it important that the boys know the difference between those who had kept themselves pure and those who had willingly defiled themselves.

"When both the northern and southern kingdoms had fallen to idolatry and the Lord God punished them with exile, not all the people were carried away. Some of the people of the Northern Kingdom escaped into the mountains and waited for the Assyrians and Babylonians to leave, which, they eventually did.

Instead of keeping the traditions of their original faith and keeping their bloodlines and lineage pure from the other inhabitants of the land, they joined themselves with whoever was willing to take them and ceased to be a distinct people. When children and grandchildren of those who had been exiled from Jerusalem to Babylon came back to rebuild what had been lost, some of the descendents of the northern kingdom tried to join back up with them.

The prophets of that time gave them the chance to return if only they would give up their foreign wives and false gods. Those people refused and went back up north, into the mountains of Samaria were they are to this day. They are no longer Jews and while they claim to worship the one true God, they mix heathen practices and traditions into their own warped concept of God," finished Matthew, who then spit like he was trying to expel the entire Samaritan people.

"Whether they do good or evil is immaterial to the fact that what they are and have become is an abomination to God."

"Sir, I have heard this story before and I have seen the desperation of those ruined people," started Jesus, who wanted to ask a question. "When Messiah comes, will he not, once again, after offering salvation to the Jewish people, try to redeem the Samaritan people along with the rest of the nations?"

Matthew regarded the young Nazarene for a moment before answering him. "I have heard that there are hints of something like that prophesied in some of the Later Prophets' prophecies, but I am not a scholar that could tell you for sure," said Matthew with a soft voice. "Tomorrow, when you accompany Lazarus to his religion classes, make sure you ask the rabbi, he will be sure to know." Signaling with his hand that the discussion was over, Matthew led the two boys up the stair and into the living quarters of the house for the night.

That night Jesus prayed while lying on the blanket provided to him by Lazarus's mother. He would have preferred going to the rooftop but figured that since he was a guest in the house, he should not burden them with additional requirements. He knew that God would hear him just fine wherever he was.

"Oh Father, thank you for the provision that you gave Micah in his time of trouble. Please Lord, help me to understand what You have planned for the redemption of the Samaritans," prayed Jesus, silently to His God. "Lord, I thank you for providing me a place to go until I can be reunited with father and mother. Help them not to be worried and help them to see your will in our being separated. Lord, help me to get the most I can get from the lesson tomorrow. I have so many questions about Your Word and Scriptures. Please bless this family and thank you for the friendship of Lazarus. Please bless my sleep and give me strength for tomorrow."

As was his custom, Jesus quieted his spirit and tried to empty his mind of the things of the world. He lay very still as he waited for the Lord to answer him and fellowship with him. His last thought before falling asleep was in the form of a question. "How could anyone think that God and His Scriptures were a drag?"

Thirty-Seven

What About the Samaritans?

Jesus and Lazarus crossed over the Cedron Brook the next morning as the sun lighted the gray sky. The boys could clearly see men extinguishing the fire lamps that lit up the Temple at night. It seemed strange to Jesus that they should go to all those lengths to light the one place that should shine from the presence of God. He thought it sad that the people preferred ritual to a relationship with God, and that He had to remove Himself from their presence because of their sinful nature.

His attention came back to the present as a Temple guard opened the gate and the boys were passed inside into the Temple. After climbing the numerous stairs to the get to the Temple grounds, the boys made their way over to the Portico of Solomon that was the usual meeting place for Lazarus' class. Waiting for them were not just the headmaster rabbi who normally taught the boys but also other rabbis and teachers who were not immediately identified.

Lazarus' teacher, Caiaphas, who looked like he had not gotten that much sleep the night before, called over the two young men of Israel. "Lazarus, I and these other men would like to speak with Jesus here alone for a while," said Caiaphas, holding the boy by the shoulders. "Have the rest of the class start where you left off yesterday and I should be able to join you in a while." With that the teacher turned the farm boy around and pointed him in the direction of the class that was now some 100 feet further down the portico than usual. With a warning look to Jesus that clearly said "watch yourself with these guys," Lazarus walked off to join his class.

Jesus faced the men as they considered him silently. Then Caiaphas came and put his arm around the boy's shoulders. "Why don't we all sit down," said the teacher, who then settled with the Nazarene boy at his side to the steps below. Jesus noticed that while one or two of the others also sat on the steps, the other five or six teachers that had been silent up to this point remained standing.

Caiaphas started out the questioning. "Just so my colleagues can be brought up to speed, I'm going to start off by asking some of the same questions I asked you yesterday," Caiaphas said softly to the boy while the others looked on. "Who was it you said who has been teaching you the doctrines of the Law and the Prophets?"

Jesus looked at the man with a wrinkled brow, wondering if the man could hear properly. "I told you that besides by parents and the weekly Sabbath lesson in the town's synagogue, I have not yet started my formal education," said Jesus. "I will start that as soon as I get back under the headmastership of Rabbi Moshe, rabbi of Nazareth."

"That's right, that's what you said," exclaimed Caiaphas, as if he just now remembered the details of the previous afternoon. "So how do you come by the understanding of the Scriptures that you showed yesterday in regard to the story of the great flood?"

"I remembered having the Scripture story read at the synagogue a few years back and I remembered what God told me regarding what had happened," answered Jesus, unaware of the raised eyebrows that came from the men in the group.

"So you have talked with God?" asked Daniel, a bald headed man with crooked teeth who wore the robes of a priest. "When was the last time you heard from the Almighty?"

"Last night when I prayed to Him," answered Jesus honestly. Conversation erupted all at once from all of the men gathered around the young boy. Soon it was as though Jesus wasn't even there in their midst as they debated back and forth on whether any one person can hear the voice of God. The men argued the point for more than an hour before they heard the voice of the boy, who had been listening to their discussions chime in with his own question.

"What about Samuel?" Jesus asked. "Before he was a prophet and before he was even as old as I am, God spoke to him." The men, who had been arguing from a remote religious viewpoint, were stunned to hear the boy answer and question them from a Scriptural point of view. The question momentarily silenced them before they all began to debate again the subject at hand. Jesus noticed that now they were talking about the Scriptural reference he had pointed out instead of what they had thought was right and was pleased that he had made some contribution to the discussion.

The conversation seemed to be dying down, with the consensus being that one could hear from God Himself if that person kept the Law down to the last letter. Turning back to question the boy further, Jesus jumped in with his own question before the men could ask anything further.

"I heard a traveler last night tell of being waylaid by robbers on the road to Jericho," began Jesus, who immediately caught the attention of the teachers and learned men. "He was eventually helped, after being ignored by numerous individuals, by a Samaritan businessman. Even though the Samaritans are cursed by God now, won't they be able to be reconciled to the one true God when Messiah comes?"

Drowning out the rest of the men who immediately started to answer, Josiah, an old and frail rabbi who had sit down when Jesus and Caiaphas did, spoke out in a startling strong voice. "The Samaritans have no place with the God of Israel. What makes you think boy, that they or any other gentile will have any place before the throne of our God?"

"My family has a copy of the writings of the prophet Isaiah, sir," answered Jesus, who was not intimidated by the hostility in Josiah's voice. "In our family devotions I remember hearing read the prophet's words,"

> *O Lord, thou art my God; I will exalt thee, I will praise thy name; for thou has done wonderful things; thy counsels of old are faithfulness and truth.*
>
> *For thou has made of a city a heap; of a defended city a ruin: a palace of strangers to be no city; it shall never be built.*
>
> *Therefore shall the strong people glorify thee, the city of the terrible nations shall fear thee.*
>
> *For thou hast been a strength to the poor, a strength to the needy in his distress, a refuge from the storm, a shadow from the heat, when the blast of the terrible ones is as a storm against the wall.*
>
> *Thou shall bring down the noise of strangers, as the heat in a dry place; even the heat with the shadow of a cloud: the branch of the terrible ones shall be brought low.*
>
> *And in this mountain shall the LORD of hosts make unto all people a feast of fat things, a feast of wines on the lees, of fat things full of marrow, of wines on the lees well refined.*

And he will destroy in this mountain the face of the covering
cast over all people, and the veil that is spread over all
nations.

He will swallow up death in victory; and the Lord GOD will
wipe away tears from off all faces; and the rebuke of his
people shall he take away from off all the earth: for the
LORD hath spoken it.

And it shall be said in that day, Lo, this is our God; we have
waited for him, and he will save us: this is the LORD; we
have waited for him, we will be glad and rejoice in his
salvation.

For in this mountain shall the hand of the LORD rest, and
Moab shall be trodden down under him, even as straw is
trodden down for the dunghill.

And he shall spread forth his hands in the midst of them, as he
that swims spreads forth his hands to swim: and he shall
bring down their pride together with the spoils of their
hands.

And the fortress of the high fort of thy walls shall he bring
down, lay low, and bring to the ground, even to the dust.

When Jesus stopped his recitation, the learned men were shocked. Only one of the men present was sure that the young boy had quoted the Scripture correctly. Balchri, a tall, hawked-nosed man in his mid-fifties stepped forward after the boy finished.

"You have quoted the prophet correctly young man; a feat that tells me that you have a future among our ranks one day," said Balchri in a formal tone that only Pharisees used. "I suspect that you could quote much more, but before that, tell me and my learned compatriots, why you think this has any bearing on the question at hand?"

"The scripture talked of the Lord hosting a banquet for all of the nations," Jesus said. "By default, wouldn't one of those nations have to be the people of Samaria?" Before Jesus could draw another breath, the men around the steps had launched into a fierce debate that lasted the rest of the afternoon. None of those present seemed to notice that the noon mealtime had come and gone. The amazing thing from Jesus' point of view was that the learned men were treating him as an equal. He not only got to listen to their questions of one another but was also allowed to ask questions of them.

Caiaphas interrupted the debate when he noticed Lazarus sitting to one side. The farmer's son's schooling was done for the day and not wanting to leave his newfound friend, had purposed to wait until Jesus was told he could go.

Caiaphas cleared his throat to suspend the conversation before talking. "I think our young friend here must go for the day, let's meet back here tomorrow morning and pick up where we have left off. Looking at Jesus, Caiaphas said, "There are still some pressing questions that need to be answered. How soon will you and your family be going back to Nazareth? Jesus turned red at the question and shrugged that he didn't know.

"Be back here tomorrow then," ordered Caiaphas. "I have some more friends who would find this discussion of some merit and I think we will invite Daniel's father-in-law Mishael, the High Priest, whom you have met." With that the group broke up and went their ways in two and threes, still debating whether God talks to Gentiles or not.

Jesus walked to the stairs with Lazarus that would take them out the gate and down the road to Bethany. Lazarus didn't speak until they were across the bridge. "Did you understand anything those men were saying?" asked the farmers boy who struggled in his own studies.

"Yes, we were discussing the writings and prophecies of the prophet Isaiah and whether God will redeem the Gentiles along with us Jews when the Messiah comes," answered Jesus as though he was talking about the difference between corn and wheat.

"If you say so," said Lazarus. "I would be bored out of my mind if I was you and got trapped listening to all of those old men argue back and forth." Before Jesus could refute the boredom remark, Lazarus pointed up the side of the mountain, toward the Garden of Gethsemane. "Look at the size of that olive tree!" the farmer's boy gasped with wide eyes. As Jesus turned to look at where his friend was pointing, Lazarus broke into a run down the road.

As Jesus looked back toward his friend, he barely heard the challenge coming from the retreating back of Lazarus. "Race you to the town!"

Thirty-Eight

Proverbs by the Firelight

"So did you find out about the Samaritan question we were talking about last night?" asked Matthew to Jesus, as the farmer's family finished with the evening meal.

"That was the subject of most of the discussion this afternoon by the rabbis and priests sir," answered Jesus to his more than generous host. "They came to the conclusion that God would redeem the Samaritans when Messiah comes, but only if they follow the Law of Moses."

"Well, that sounds about right," Matthew agreed. "Were there others besides Lazarus's teacher?"

"There were about ten other men who sat around and talked," said Jesus. "They wanted to question me about how I know so much Scripture, but they kept getting side-tracked on different issues."

"I see. Well I hope you have minded your manners in front of such austere and holy men as those with whom you have been keeping company," said Matthew, who was slightly troubled by the attention being paid to this young man from Nazareth.

"Oh yes sir," exclaimed Jesus. "There are so many questions I have for them, but at times, it's hard to get a word in edgewise."

Getting up from the table, the farmer stretched and moved toward his sleeping room. Looking back over his shoulder, he said, "You boys get ready for the council fire. We will be going in a few minutes." With that Jesus and Lazarus got up from the table and went to wash their hands and faces and get their yarmulkes.

The fire meeting that night was more traditional than the previous night. There were no visitors and no guest of honor. The elders of Bethany judged a few disputes and heard the news of the world. Plans for the next festival were discussed and it was mentioned by several of the men that Zaccheus, the local tax collector, was due to come by within the next few days.

At the end of the business portion of the meeting, the young men, including Lazarus and Jesus were asked to come and sit closer to the fire. There were about 15 teenagers present, ranging from 14 to 19 years of age.

"What were your studies today?" asked Joash, who, as the senior elder of the town was responsible for this portion of the counsel fire. "Did you study the Law, History, Prophets or Writings?"

The oldest of the boys, Simon, stood to his feet. "The older boys studied Ezekiel while the younger are learning about what took place after the flood in the Law."

"Very good," said Joash. "So tell me, what have you learned that is practical and can be used today?"

At this question, all of the boys stood to their feet. Starting with Simon and ending with Jesus, each of the boys shared a truth learned and pondered over the course of the day. The boys were not allowed to repeat what they had previously recited nor could they use what another boy had recently used.

"The knowledge of God is the beginning of wisdom," exclaimed Simon, who then turned to the next oldest and waited for his words of wisdom, most of which, all of those present knew, came from the proverbs of Solomon. In an unbroken chain, each boy that night was prepared with his proverb. At last only two young men remained. "Hear my son, and accept my sayings and the years of your life will be many," quoted Lazarus, who worried at times that God might construe his complaining as dishonoring to his parents and thus shorten his life. With Lazarus' proverb complete all eyes, young and old focused on the newest addition to the nightly fire.

Thinking about all that he had heard and learned that day about his own people, the Jews and their relationship with other peoples of the earth, Jesus said to them, *"Do not judge so that you will not be judged. For in the way you judge, you will be judged; and by your standard of measure, it will be measured to you."* As Jesus finished, the men around the fire pondered the words of the young men and nodding moved to dismiss them for the evening.

"One moment, Jesus," said Joash from across the fire. As the rest of the boys quickly disappeared back into the fringes behind their fathers, Jesus turned back around to face the town's senior elder.

"I have been attending fireside councils since I was your age. I have heard all of the proverbs recited in that time," stated Joash. "I have never heard the words that you have spoken tonight. Do they come from the Scriptures and if so, who was the prophet?"

"No sir, I did not quote any prophet or writing from the Scriptures," said Jesus. "I made up the proverb from what

I think I have learned today from my time with the rabbis at the Temple."

"I see," said Joash. "If we are not to judge, then how will any disputes be settled?"

"There is only one judge, sir," answered Jesus immediately. "The Lord God is He, as we all know. It is only by asking of His knowledge and wisdom that we can have any knowledge or wisdom. All such things truly only come from Him," finished the boy from Nazareth. Nodding his understanding of the explanation and wondering about the boy's understanding of such things at such an early age, Joash dismissed Jesus and the others for the evening. There was no discussion, no "farewells" or "what are you doing tomorrows". Each man of Israel walked home, quietly, alone, in wonder and in thought.

Thirty-Nine

Can All Be Jews?

"Rabbi Caiaphas," Jesus said, immediately after the two met for the third day in a row early the next morning. "I was at the council fire down in Bethany last night, with Lazarus and his father. I got to thinking about all that was discussed here yesterday and the wisdom of the proverbs that were recited last night. Any way, I have question for you and the other teachers and priests."

"Be careful, Caiaphas," said Malachi, a fat man dressed in very fine robes. He had been introduced to Jesus yesterday as a rabbi and Pharisee of a synagogue on the south side of Jerusalem. "The boy will invoke a discussion that will take the rest of the day to work through like he did yesterday." At this comment all of the men gathered around the young Galilean carpenter's apprentice burst into laughter. Jesus laughed with them until the laughter died down.

"Before he asks his question of us, let's get some information from him," said Ezra, a newcomer to the group that morning. He was the chief scribe at the Temple, and people who knew the Scriptures as well as he had heard this boy knew them were of particular interest to him.

"Jesus, what does your father do and are you following him in his trade?" asked the scribe.

"My father is a carpenter and I am apprenticed to him," answered Jesus in a straightforward manner that almost disarmed the older gentleman. "I have already started to handle projects myself in our family business."

"So you are not the son of a Pharisee, scribe, or priest?" asked Zacharias, who was also a scribe. He had come to Jerusalem for Passover from Qumran, where he was in charge of a community of scribes that did nothing but copy and preserve the Scriptures. "How is it that you have come to know the Scriptures so well?"

"What I read and hear of the Scriptures I remember, sir," said Jesus. "It's almost as if each and every word becomes a part me." Before any of the other men could ask any more questions, Jesus asked his. "Sirs, allow me to ask my question," started Jesus, who then kept going before the others could object. "Does the redemption that God will bring through the Messiah apply only to Jews? What of God's promise to Abraham?" asked Jesus, looking from one face to another.

Raising his voice above the rest, before all semblance of order would be lost, Balchri asked a qualifying question of Jesus that silenced the others. "Which promise do you refer to, young man?" asked the hawked-nosed Pharisee.

"God promised Abraham that all the nations of the earth would be blessed through him," said Jesus. "What is this blessing? And how will God deliver this blessing to those nations?" For the rest of the morning the men bandied back and forth their opinions of how the Gentiles would be blessed.

Josiah argued that God would bless all the peoples of the earth through the Jews. "Those people will get the portion that God wants them to have through us," he said tapping his chest with the index finger of his right hand. "When they start keeping the Law that the Jews follow, they will begin to be blessed." While some of the men frowned, most of them nodded their heads in agreement. God had come to them, the Jews, and revealed Himself to them. If the world were to be blessed they would have to become even as the Jews were in order for them to have any standing in the Law.

"So what you're saying is that in order for the Gentiles to be blessed, they would have to become Jews in every way?" asked Jesus who was also frowning, not sure if he agreed with the statement or not. "Is that possible?"

Once more a voice rose above the others as the volume began to rise. "Before we entertain such a question, could we not break for the noon meal," asked the very plump Malachi. "I found it very hard to concentrate yesterday when we skipped the meal."

"Very well," said Caiaphas. "I will have the trumpeter sound three times in the next hour to signal for our return. Is that enough time?"

Each man gave his assent and then parted company to return to their dwellings. Caiaphas turned to Jesus to ask if he would share in his mealtime, but the boy had already walked away toward the class that was also breaking up. The headmaster looked after the carpenter's apprentice as he sat down beside his friend, Lazarus. The farmer's son untied a pouch that had been tied to his belt. Caiaphas saw that the two had brought some fruit and dried figs and were sharing for the time allotted them to eat.

Caiaphas walked away to his own lunch with a priest named Annas, who was in line for the High Priestship. Caiaphas had been talking with the man about his daughter, whom the Pharisee thought was very beautiful. Maybe today, he thought, I will ask for her.

After lunch the men returned and took up the debate again. Unlike the day before, no consensus could be reached and the men on each side in the matter dug in more and more as the afternoon progressed. Leading the side that argued that blessing could only come from obedience to the Law was Josiah.

"Without the Law and without the shedding of blood that is done right here in this Temple we have no access to God. Without the sheep, goats, bulls, and rams being offered in sacrifice to God, there is no remission of sins," argued the old Pharisee vehemently. "If the rest of the world wants to be included under the covenant that Moses brought down from God Himself, they must keep all of the Law."

"Prophets like Isaiah, Jeremiah, and Ezekiel claimed that no one could do that," said a small voice on the opposite side of Josiah. "Those prophets spoke for God and with God's authority. If we can't do it, what makes us think that the Gentiles can do it?" asked Jesus. "Those prophets whom you named spoke to a generation who had fallen away from the worship of the one true God," said a newcomer to the conversation. "I believe today we have accomplished all of the Law by building God's Temple anew and by keeping all of what is in the Law," said Gamaliel, who had been listening to the argument silently for the past hour.

"Rabban, how good of you to join us. Is our High Priest also going to join into the conversation?" asked Daniel, who had sided himself with Josiah and saw the comments that the most respected teacher in all of Judaism had made as a boon to their cause.

"He begs all of your pardon. He has been detained this afternoon, even though he had promised to set aside time," said Gamaliel. "He asks if it would be possible that we all meet back here tomorrow."

"I will be here for sure tomorrow, respected teacher, but I cannot speak for everyone," said Caiaphas. "Young man, will you be able to come tomorrow or will you have to go back to building shelves and chests?"

"As far as I know I will be able to come back, sirs," said Jesus who then plunged ahead with one last question. "If Jew and Gentiles alike are only justified to God by the Law of Moses, then how was Abraham justified by his faith? Abraham was born more than 430 years before Moses had his first encounter with the Lord."

The rest of the afternoon was spent debating the subject at hand. There were no winners and no losers. The Pharisees, scribes, priests, and rabbis were at their best in this kind of debate. To Jesus it was fascinating to hear these learned men discuss the very Scripture he loved. He added very little to the rest of the conversation. The boy from Galilee listened to the questions and considered the answers. He knew that he would have to ask God Himself if any of them were right.

After all, he mused to himself that night as he was running down the hill ahead of Lazarus, why wonder about questions that you don't have the answers for and go on in ignorance when you could approach God, who after all held all the answers.

That night's council fire was short and for the most part taken up by a land sale between two families. The proverbs that were recited by the young men were all ones that everyone had heard before and no new thoughts were provoked. For the most part Jesus remained quiet and thoughtful. His mind was far away, up the mountainside where questions of redemption and reconciliation with God had been discussed, argued and explored for most of the day.

That night, before falling asleep, he once again talked to his Heavenly Father. Jesus knew for sure that God willed that no one should perish but that all would come to the knowledge of Him. He was sure because God had reassured him in his prayers.

Jesus was unsure of how to convince the teachers and priest that God wanted more than just a mindless homage to the Law. As the boy lay there in the room with his friend snoring away in the opposite corner, he began to cry as the God of the Universe shared His need for fellowship with His creation.

"Oh Father, empower me to reveal your heart and mind to this world," Jesus said out loud, not even bothering to hold to himself his prayers to his God. "Help me to be the instrument of Your will." The carpenter's apprentice fell asleep that night in fellowship with the God he loved. While at peace with the answers that God had provided him, he was also prepared with new questions to steer the conversation the next day in a new direction.

Forty

Dual Citizenship

With Passover done, Raul only needed one more thing to make this visit to Jerusalem perfect. This was the eighth day after his son had been born, which meant that today was the day his son would be named and circumcised. With the help of the centurion, Gaius, his son would also this day become a citizen of Rome, from the city of Tarsus. With the help of Rufus, one of Gaius's soldiers, Leah and his son were not dead from the traumatic circumstances of childbirth in the wild.

His friend Gamaliel, with whom he and his family were staying, had said that he would be on hand this morning at the Temple for the ceremony. What would take place would forever mark the new baby boy as a Jew and Israelite and child of the covenant that God made with Abraham.

When Raul, Leah, and the babe reached the court of the Gentiles, Rabban Gamaliel, greatest rabbi and Pharisee the Jewish nation had known for hundreds of years, met them.

"Peace be with you, Raul, and to you, Leah," said the scholar and teacher. "This is a momentous day."

"Peace be unto you revered teacher," Raul said while bowing low. "I only come to seek your limitless and bountiful wisdom and knowledge."

"Stop it, Raul," laughed Gamaliel. "It's bad enough when people talk to me like that for real. If you're ready, the High Priest is waiting." The man had been gifted in the Torah from his youth and his understanding in even the most obscure passages of the revered scriptures was unsurpassed.

Together, the group made their way to the Court of Women, where the ceremony would take place. Circumcisions and other ceremonies that would involve women had to be done there because only men were allowed beyond the Court of Women and only priests were allowed past the altar of burnt offering and inside the Holy Place. Only the High Priest, and he only once a year, was allowed to enter the Holy of Holies, a section of the Holy Place that had been sectioned off by a curtain.

The High Priest, Mishael, was waiting for them in the Court of Women with two of his Levite helpers. They were standing by a square stone table off to one side of the court when the family from Tarsus and the revered teacher approached.

"Gamaliel, peace be unto you, introduce me to your friends, so that we all might be friends together," exclaimed Mishael, who, in his robes of office looked every inch of what a High Priest should look.

"High Priest of Israel, peace be unto you, let me introduce Raul of Tarsus, who was born in Bethany and now holds the position of rabbi," said Gamaliel. "He was appointed to the post by your predecessor a few years back and is doing a wonderful job. He was telling me that he is presently leading over 25 Greeks in the conversion process to Judaism."

"That is wonderful," replied the High Priest. "Our faith grows every day and we welcome in new proselytes from all over the world." Motioning one of his assistances to come forward, the High Priest took a bundle from the man's hands and laid it on the stone table. Picking up the ceremonial knife that had been wrapped inside the cloth that had made the bundle, he handed the instrument to his other assistant. Turning back to his guest, the High Priest explained.

"Shireck will go and cleanse the ceremonial knife in the Holy Water that bubbles up from a creek just outside the Holy Place," Mishael said as he made a vague gesture with his hand toward the Holy Place. "While we wait for him to return, may I have the male child?"

Leah, who had been cradling the child near her breast, handed the baby to his father who then handed him to the High Priest.

"What is to be the child's name?" asked the high priest to Raul as the former held the child high in the air, as a wave offering to God.

"His name shall be called Saul, an honored name in the tribe of Benjamin," Raul said. "Before God, his mother, my friend Rabban Gamaliel and the High Priest, I give him into the Almighty's service to do with as He pleases." The naming completed; Mishael laid the child on the cloth that had held the knife and reached out to Shireck who had just returned with the dripping instrument. In a swift, practiced movement, the High Priest removed the foreskin of the child. As the child wailed, Mishael allowed Leah, who had jumped forward at the sound of her child's cry, to recover Saul and spread the balm that would speed healing over the cut area.

"Remember to offer the appropriate sacrifice," Mishael reminded Leah. "I must be going," said the high priest. "I'm scheduled for a bar Mitzvah in a couple of minutes. Could I have a private word with you, Gamaliel? And, with you too, Raul?"

"Oh course," chimed the Rabban and rabbi together.

"Leah, why don't you go and purchase the sacrifice needed for the redemption of our first born," said Raul to his wife. "I'll be along in a moment." Leah walked off with her son Saul, happy to have the opportunity to walk in the Temple grounds while the sycophants of the priest busied themselves with the next task that their master would have to perform.

"There is an exceptional young man among us who is the marvel of the teachers of the Temple," said High Priest Mishael when the three were alone. "They say he is from Nazareth, yet know one has ever heard of his parents. Gamaliel, and uh, you also Raul, if you have time, perhaps you could go over to the Portico of Solomon and examine him yourselves? I have been invited over myself and have scheduled in a few minutes this afternoon."

"I would be honored to accompany you this afternoon to see and question this boy," said Gamaliel, who was at once intrigued by the situation.

"I cannot come this afternoon, I'm afraid," said Raul. "I have a previous appointment. Besides, if the High Priest and the Rabban of Israel can't judge correctly, then we are all in serious danger." With a hardy, good-natured laugh, the party split up and the High Priest climbed the stairs toward the altar of burnt offerings and the Holy Place.

Gamaliel turned to his friend before going back to his place of study in the Temple. "My friend, I offer you a gift," stated the Rabban with a smile on his face.

"Oh please, Gamaliel, your hospitality and presence here today has been gift enough," pleaded the over-wrought rabbi of Tarsus.

"In truth, I have only one gift to give to this child of yours, since being wise and having knowledge in the Scriptures has not led to wealth," said Gamaliel, laughing at his friend's discomfort. "I offer to him, and to you and Leah, my services as his personal teacher when he comes of age. He will be, if you accept, my responsibility to teach in the ways of our ancestors." Raul was speechless. His friend was the greatest rabbi and Pharisee in all the land. Any student of his would gain enormous prestige upon completion of this master's school.

"I accept gratefully, but on the condition that he proves worthy to be such a great master's student," replied Raul.

"I will see you tonight, then, and what a feast we shall have," said Gamaliel, who then turned a left toward his study chamber at the back of the temple grounds.

Raul, Leah, and Saul left the Temple area after offering the appropriate sacrifice of two turtledoves at the altar. They made for the Roman garrison that was just outside the gates of the Temple to see if they could locate Gaius. It so happened that the centurion was on duty when they walked inside the garrison. They were taken quickly to the official who recorded births, a small man with ink stains on his hands.

"I met this couple on my way here from Rome, up north on the coast, south of Tyre," Gaius told the man as way of introduction. "As you can see, they have had a baby boy, which I was present to witness and to help out in some small way." The official looked bored with the story and gestured with a wave of his hand for the proud centurion to complete his story.

"These people are from Tarsus, in the Cilicia region. Their child is Roman by birth and they wish to register his birth as such," said Gaius, who then bent over the small table where the minor official worked. He smiled, and it was not a pleasant smile. His voice was quiet but hard as flint. "That's not going to be a problem is it, magistrate?" Getting the point immediately, the Roman functionary straightened in his seat and smiled at the Jewish couple that had the powerful, cruel centurion as a friend. "Of course not, no problem at all," he said. "Let me just get the parchment, quill and ink and the birth rolls and we'll be done in no time."

Forty-One

Search

"Where could he be?" Joseph asked himself for what must have been the thousandth time. After arriving back in the City of David, he and his wife had been looking for their son for three days. They had looked everywhere they thought a twelve-year-old boy would be. They had also looked in places they hoped a boy – or a man for that matter – would never be.

They had looked through the market the first day, reasoning that he would need to eat and that's where people got food. After a full day of looking for, asking about, describing in detail, and crying over, their lost son, they had checked into an inn for the night, thankful for the money Joshua had given them. The inn was not crowded, most of the Passover crowd was gone and Mary and Joseph were assigned a room overlooking the street; a room usually reserved for a traveling merchant or religious personage.

They would have kept looking for him at night in their hometown but this was the big city. They did not feel safe in Jerusalem and were not familiar with the rules peculiar to the city. They would stand out as the visitors and simple small town folk that they were and would be marked for robbery or worse. Joseph thought of the robbery attempt on the way down from the north in the region of Samaria and the possibility that his son would have to face such men alone was disheartening. That thought brought more visions of doom than anything else did that day and they went to bed exhausted and broken hearted, fearing the worst.

The second day they had scoured the seedier parts of the city. Swallowing their pride and dignity they turned to questioning beggars and prostitutes. Feeling more confident about dealing with the beggars, Joseph and Mary approached a man who appeared to be blind, standing on a street corner a few streets down from the temple. He was thrusting an earthenware bowl out in front of himself as if to give something away rather than receive a gift of charity. As Joseph approached with Mary a few steps behind him, the man sensed their presence and almost broke Joseph's nose as he thrust the bowl straight into his face.

"Alms," cried the beggar. "Alms for the blind and poor in spirit." Joseph, instinctively knowing that if they would get any information from this man he would have to donate to his cause reached for the moneybag tied at his waist.

"Hello, have you seen, ah, well, ah," Joseph said mumbling the last as he realized what he said. "Have you heard of a lost boy who ..." Joseph stopped talking as he felt for the drawstring and was momentarily surprised and then enraged to find the beggars fingers already there. The thief was deftly opening the knots that held it closed. Joseph took a step back and slapped at the man's suddenly strong arms to release his grip from around the sack of money. When the beggar felt the callused hand of the northern carpenter come into contact with his arm, his eyes, seemingly by the act of a miracle popped open and with a desperate look around, fled down a previously unnoticed alley without looking back. Joseph and Mary looked at one another with looks of disbelief.

"If this is the typical behavior of the people on this side of the city," said Mary as she watched here husband retie the money bag to his rope belt, "we will never find our son."

"We will find him," said Joseph unconvincingly. "We must have faith."

"Well I don't think we can trust the beggars," said Mary as the couple continued to walk and search. "After all, how are we supposed to describe Jesus to a blind man?"

Turning a corner, the couple spotted a veiled woman, alone in a doorway, halfway down an abandoned alleyway. Taking a deep breath, they approached the woman, not really knowing what to say. This time Mary took the lead, with her husband in the rear. It would not do to give this woman the impression that they were there for regular business as opposed to their real cause. The woman, Mary noticed, was much older than what she appeared to be from a distance. After a few comments to the lady and listening to the prostitute's reply, Mary turned and fled, passing her husband and racing out of the alley as the harlot laughed raucously in her wake. Joseph, not knowing what had happened, turned and went after his wife; more laughter following him as he turned out of the alley in the direction his wife had gone.

"What happened?" asked Joseph who noticed that his wife's face was beet red and her eyes brimmed with tears. "What did she say? Had she seen him?"

"She said that she would lay with me or you or both of us together if that's what we wanted," said Mary as she regained some composure. "When I asked her about Jesus she said that she may have seen him. When I described him to her she just laughed.

"What did she say? Had she seen him?" asked Joseph again, unprepared for the answer his wife would give him.

"She said that …" Mary paused and then went on. "She said that she made young teenage boys into men every day and that Jesus fit the description of every one of them."

"Oh no, Mary," said Joseph to his wife. "Jesus would not go with a woman like that."

"I know," said the boy's mother. "It's a horrible thought to know that women like that prey on young boys. At about mid-morning, they came upon a group of people congregating in the mouth of an alleyway in the southern part of the city. Approaching the crowd, they identified two men walking around the alley as Roman legionnaires. As they got closer, they noticed the ripped and bloodied tunic of an old man lying face down in the dirt, clearly dead. Panning and working the crowd for information, Joseph and Mary quickly learned that the man had been beaten and robbed by a group of young zealots that had been terrorizing that part of town since before the Passover week had begun.

"Those zealots are growing at an alarming rate, especially among the young men," said one old woman, with a shake of her head. "They hate the Romans and want them to leave. They commit these acts because they can't get the people to rise up as one against them."

"Don't the young ones know that the Messiah will be here soon?" another old lady asked the searching couple. "My mother told me before she died over ten years ago that she had seen the Messiah and that it would only be a matter of time before he set things aright." Joseph and Mary drifted away from the old woman, knowing that the longer they stayed, the more daylight would be burned.

"There's only one reason the legionnaires are at this scene and concerned," another old woman stated as Mary and Joseph walked away. "It's because the one who's dead was a tax collector for the governor. Can't walk the streets at all anymore."

Mary and Joseph continued looking around the streets for their son, but now they seldom spoke to anyone and the conversation between themselves had petered down to the basics. Their spirits tumbled as they realized that if their boy had become lost in this part of the city, just about the worst imagined things possible could have happened to him. As they made their way back to the inn that evening, despair's grip left a knot of futility in the pits of their stomachs, the candle flame of their hope was starting to flicker. Tired and hungry, they had no appetite and went to sleep that night knowing that if they didn't find their son by this time the following day he was probably dead.

Joseph had an inspiration that night, and by morning he and Mary were invigorated with new hope. "I have it," said Joseph. "I asked myself, if I were all alone in a strange city, where would I go?

"You would go to the local carpenter," said Mary, answering the question for him. "I should have thought of that. How many times did we stop at strange towns on the way to Egypt and then on the way back? You must know every carpenter and tradesman from here to Alexandria."

"I imagine there is more than one here in Jerusalem," said Joseph. "The tradesmen all have their shops on the south-west side of town."

"Let's go," said Mary. "With God's blessing, we should be able find him by noon." Joseph found out, too late, that his reasoning was flawless; it was the conclusion of his reasoning that was in error. They had started with the carpenters, there were several, as this was a big city. Back home Joseph was 'the' carpenter, but here there were more than a dozen.

The first man they approached was a furniture maker. His shop displayed only one of each of the wares he made. He was working on a chair when Joseph approached, this time with Mary waiting outside.

"Hello friend," said Joseph. "Have you seen a young man, twelve years old, in the past few days?"

"No, I haven't," said the man as he looked Joseph up and down. "I see by the splinter marks and stain on your hands that you're no stranger to woodwork."

"I'm the carpenter of Nazareth," replied Joseph. "My boy got left behind after Passover. My wife and I thought he might have come this way, to the trade areas."

"I haven't been out of the shop, it seems in days," said the man who felt sorry for Joseph. "Let me call my son and see if he's seen any new kids around lately."

"Jesus!" called the Jerusalem carpenter. "Jesus, get out here."

"Your son's name is Jesus?" asked Joseph. "That's my boys name also."

"You don't say?" said the carpenter. "Well, it is a popular name, I suppose. Here he comes." A boy about fifteen years of age with light brown hair and green eyes approached. "Yeah, Dad?" he said. "You called? I was just getting ready to sand that plank."

"Have you seen any new kids around from out of town in the past couple of days?" asked the city carpenter. "He has the same name as you."

"I saw a kid about three days ago come through here," said Jesus. "But he was with someone who looked like his father. Does that help any?"

"No," said Joseph shaking his head. "But thanks anyway. I'll try the next few shops."

"I'll be on the lookout for him," said the carpenter. "May God give you peace and success."

"The same to you," said Joseph who turned and walked out the door. Mary, with a hopeful look in her eyes looked at her husband as he emerged from the carpenter's shop but when she saw the downtrodden look in his face, she knew he had no new information. They visited six more shops that morning, but to no avail. Their oldest son had not been to any of them nor had any members of the carpenters' community seen him. The last family had taken pity on Joseph and Mary and had invited them to the midday meal of bread, nuts and cheese. While still sick with worry, the couple was hungry and thankfully ate what had been offered. After they had eaten, they thanked their host and blessed them and their business, then left to continue the search.

When they didn't find him with any of the carpenters, they then went to the other tradesmen. After hours of searching they knew that Joseph's conclusion about him going to that part of town had been wrong. It was Mary, that evening, at the end of her rope, and with no other alternatives, who suggested that they go to the temple.

"Let's go to the Temple first thing in the morning," she said to her husband. "We can pray for Jesus safety and we can ask the High Priest if he has seen him."

"Good idea," said Joseph. "After all, the High Priest should remember him from his bar-Mitsvah." As they traveled up the mountainside and made their way through the sheep gate into the temple area, Joseph wondered what the boy's real father would have to say to them. Being in this place, it was easy to think about the boy's father. Joseph grimaced with the additional burden that he had failed the father as much as he had failed himself.

Forty-Two

The Will of God

As the group gathered the next morning, Jesus was careful to be patient until all arrived. Gamaliel arrived on time with a new face on his left-hand side and a face that Jesus knew quite well on his right.

Striding along with his friend and the High Priest, Raul felt honored to be asked to participate in what looked like a discussion with the greatest minds in all of Judaism. He wondered about the boy when they stopped before the young man and was even more puzzled when the High Priest and Gamaliel both greeted the lad by his first name. At that moment the rest of the contingent arrived and Caiaphas once more took charge of the meeting.

"I see all of us have returned today and we are honored to have High Priest Mishael and Rabban Gamaliel with us," said Caiaphas in what was to Jesus, a very formal tone. Turning to Jesus the Temple schoolmaster said, "I see that woodworking has also taken a back seat to the things of God." Jesus smiled at the man and bowed his head at being recognized in such an auspicious crowd. Then without being asked, the boy spoke.

"Sirs, I am just a very new young man in all the ways of the Jewish people. While I know Scripture and enjoy sharing with all of you the mysteries of God, I would like you to answer me two questions today."

"Will the answering of two questions take all day?" asked Mishael, who thought it strange that the rest of the men had not broken out into laughter. Turning to Gamaliel, who was busy waiting for the boy's question, the High Priest asked, "What questions could a boy so young ask that could possibly take all day?"

Holding up his hand to silence the High Priest, as he would one of his students without even thinking of the breach of etiquette, the Rabban of Israel whispered, "Sometimes it's out of the mouth of babes that some of the best wisdom comes."

"Sirs," Jesus began. "What is the will of God for this world? And what was His purpose in making the covenants with Abraham and Moses?" For a moment in time after the question was asked, every man present could hear the sizzling of the meat as it was sacrificed on the bronze altar more than 300 feet away. Then each man spoke at once and the debate was on for the third day in a row.

Mishael did not immediately join in the debate, as his mouth kept opening and closing while he looked in awe at the boy in front of him. His friend Gamaliel, whom he was a moment ago going to chastise for what amounted to an insult, had told him that this young man was a Nazarene carpenter's apprentice. He remembered the family because he had given permission just a few days ago for this same boy to start studying as a man of Israel.

His thoughts were interrupted as his son-in-law, Daniel, asked him a question of sacrifice and the High Priest entered the conversation. Lunch was again skipped that day as the sun climbed and then started its way toward the sea to the west.

Jesus for his part mostly listened as the men discussed what the will of God was for all of mankind. He prayed silently and thanked his God for the questions that had provoked so much fresh thought about the God that they all served.

By late afternoon, the conversation and debate had not slowed at all. Even fat Malachi gave no indication that he was suffering from lack of food as the day wore on. Jesus spotted Lazarus sitting on the steps of Solomon's Portico about 20 feet away, waiting for him patiently.

Not wanting to disrupt the discussion that had finally forced the men to send for the Holy Scriptures to read again what God had said to Abraham and to Moses, Jesus slipped away and sat down next to his friend.

"It looks like they are going to be awhile tonight," said Jesus. "Why don't you go ahead down the hill and I will follow as soon as I can."

"Okay," said Lazarus, who despite his best efforts looked bored. "I'll tell my mom to leave some food out for you if you don't get back in time for supper." Standing up, Lazarus took one more look at the group of men who had assembled in the Temple courtyard. "You really understand what they are saying and talking about?"

"Yes I do," said Jesus with a laugh and smile. "You'll have to take my word for it though. If I explained it to you right now, you would miss supper along with me."

"No thanks to that," said Lazarus with a smile of his own as he turned to go. "I will miss our nightly race though. I was going to beat you like I wish I could beat Martha when she starts nagging."

Forty-Three

Reunion

Joseph and Mary looked around the huge courtyard of the Temple, seeking a friendly or familiar face. The last three days had taken their toll on the couple and with the fear that they had lost their son weighing them down, both looked haggard and worn.

"Look over there," said Mary, pointing to the south end of the Portico of Solomon. "Isn't that the High Priest? He knows what Jesus looks like and he knows us from the bar-Mitzvah. Let's go ask him if he has seen or heard anything from our boy." The couple made their way over to the crowded porch and began to climb some of the steps to get to the High Priest. It was then that they heard the voice.

"I believe that God loves the entire world so much that He would do anything to save it," said Jesus as he talked with the teachers, Pharisees, and priests who made up the crowd.

"Jesus," screamed Mary. For Joseph's part, he stood amazed at how simple it was to find the boy in the end. He was also amazed that Jesus was in the company of what appeared to be the greatest minds in all of Judaism.

"Hello, Mother and Father," said Jesus looking up at them after all conversation was halted by the loud, wailing voice of the almost hysterical mother.

"Son, your father and I have been looking for you for three days," said Mary, after she had hugged her son and was assured that he had no injuries. "Why are you so calm and nonchalant, as if it's nothing to put us through this? We were so worried for you. And here you treat us as though nothing has happened."

"Why were you searching for me all over this big city?" asked Jesus, who was uncomfortable with the attention being paid to him by his parents in front of the teachers. "Didn't you know that I would be here in my Father's house attending to His business?"

Turning to the teachers and priests Jesus said, "My parents are here and want me to go, please excuse me now." With a quick glance back at his ragged and haggard looking parents, Jesus repeated himself in an almost inaudible voice, "I really have to go." Looking at his stunned parents, Jesus walked over to where they were and led them to the gate that would take them out of the temple and put them on the road to Bethany.

"Did you get a room for the night here in Jerusalem?" asked the calm carpenter's apprentice who couldn't understand why his parents were so upset. He really had wanted to stay and finish the conversation and topic that he had been involved in with the teachers. To question his parents was one thing but to openly defy them was altogether another proposition. In the end, Jesus knew that there would be another day and other conversations with some of these men. He submitted to Joseph and Mary because that was what God expected him to do. And to do the will of the Father was what Jesus strived to do more than do what he wanted to. In the end, it was more simple and satisfying to the young man of Israel.

"Where have you spent the nights, Jesus?" asked Joseph who was still feeling uneasy about some of the quizzical looks given to him by the crowd of learned men after the "Father's business" remark that Jesus had so casually flipped out. "Have you been in the Temple the whole time?"

"Remember the kid who ran us over in the Temple the day of my bar-Mitzvah?" asked Jesus, by way of answering his earthly father's question. "I came back here to the Temple the day you guys left for the north to see what his school was all about. When I couldn't find you or any of the others that were in our travel party after the school had let out, he invited me to stay at his house at night until you came back for me."

"Where is that and what is your friends name?" asked Mary, who was still floored by the casualness and calmness of her son whom she had thought just minutes before was surely dead. "Where does your friend live?"

"His name is Lazarus, Mother. I told you this, remember?" said Jesus. "He lives in Bethany, just down the mountain from here at this gate. Come on, I want you to meet him again and his family."

"Wait a minute," said Joseph, whose heart was still beating so loud he could hear the thumping in his chest. Events to him felt like they were happening just a little too fast and he just wanted to stop and sort things out. Jesus stopped and looked at the carpenter with a quizzical look.

"We can't just barge into their house and expect them to offer us hospitality," said Joseph finally after taking a few deep breaths. "We will just have to get a room tonight at the inn where your mother and I have been staying and then leave for Nazareth tomorrow morning."

"Lazarus and his family are expecting me," Jesus said to his parents. "If I don't go back there tonight they will be worried that something has happened to me."

"Well we certainly wouldn't want anyone worrying about you now, would we," said Joseph as he shook his head and rolled his eyes. "Did you ever think that we, your parents, would be as worried?"

"Yes I did, Father," said Jesus lowering his head. "There was just nothing I could do about it. I'm sorry that you had to look so long for me. If I were you, I would have come straight to the Temple. After all, where else would I be? I had no money and no idea at all how to get to our relatives in Bethlehem. Even the beggars know to come to the Temple if you are hungry and more than likely someone will take pity on you and feed you."

"Never mind that now, young man," said Mary as she rubbed her oldest son's head. "Take us to these friends of yours. I imagine that we need to thank them for the care that they have shown you these past few days."

Forty-Four

If Ever You're This Way Again

During the whole trip to Bethany, Jesus talked nonstop of his experiences and adventures since being separated from his parents. Joseph felt a wisp of remorse upon hearing that Jesus had gone to his first council fire with another man and father in a town not his home. Jesus recounted to them the tail of the Good Samaritan and the discussions that he and the teachers had about the status of the Gentiles as concerned the Messiah.

"I have heard more than once in the last ten to fifteen years that the Messiah even now walks the earth," said Mary looking at her son very closely. Some say he was born twelve years ago, while others went to their graves thanking God that the Messiah had come in their time."

"The teachers never mentioned that once," said Jesus. "I think most of them just like the 'idea' of the Messiah. From what I saw going on at the Temple, there will be a reckoning if the Messiah shows up any time soon."

Mary and Joseph said little more the rest of the way to Bethany. Mary looked at her son as she tucked away the image of her son answering and being answered by the great teachers and priest at the Temple. Some things and events that had happened in her life she would never forget and she knew that this was one of them.

Jesus introduced his family to Matthew and his wife, Mary, and their three children, Lazarus, Mary, and Martha. Mary cried in delight when she found out that Jesus' mother's name and hers were the same and immediately claimed the carpenter's wife as a long lost aunt. The Nazarene family was invited in and as it turned out was just in time for the evening meal.

"I just knew this would be his last night with us," said Mary as she ran her hand through Jesus' hair. "I fixed a young, tender lamb for tonight as a going away present for him."

After the meal and much conversation, Matthew indicated to Joseph and the two boys that it was time for them to go to the nightly fire. "You, Joseph, will be a special guest tonight as your son was a couple of nights ago," said the farmer as he rose from the table. "I image you will have much pride as your son tells the council of a proverb he has learned today.

"Yes," said Joseph. "It will be good to hear him speak in the presence of other men."

"Although," said Matthew. "From what I have heard and witnessed these past few days, it is he who will do the teaching and we who will do the learning."

Joseph was indeed the guest of honor that night and was again shocked when Jesus quoted the entire Psalm of David as he prayed to the Lord, one shepherd to another. As Jesus quoted the Scripture, Joseph couldn't help but think of other shepherds who had come down from the hills one night, not far from where he was tonight. They had come to see the young babe now grown into this Scripture-quoting young man. Joseph wondered if he would see the day when

God fulfilled the things that had been said about the young man he called his son.

Jesus quoted,

> *The Lord is my Shepherd, I lack for nothing. He makes me to*
> *lie down in green pastures and leads me to refreshing*
> *springs of water. He restores my soul.*
> *He leads me in the paths of righteousness for His name sake.*
> *Even though I walk through the valley of the shadow of death,*
> *I will fear no evil for He is with me.*
> *His rod and his staff comfort me. You, O Lord, prepare a*
> *table before me in the presence of my enemies. You have*
> *anointed my head with oil and my cup overflows.*
> *Surely goodness and mercy will follow me all the days of my life*
> *and I will abide in the house of the Lord forever.*

Since Jesus was the last to quote his learned saying for the evening, the meeting broke up soon after and all greeted Joseph and said goodbye to the two from Nazareth and wished them safety and God's mercies as they traveled home.

When they got back to the home of Matthew, Mary and the two girls were on the roof patio talking and visiting. The men and boys joined them and soon the adults were gone into a world of conversation that while it seems extremely interesting to them, bored the children to tears. Soon, Martha had left to go clean up the plates and food that was still on the table from dinner. She tried to awaken her sister, who had fallen asleep listening to their parents speak, but was unable to and left shaking her head and complaining to any who could hear her that she was mistreated and had to do all the work herself.

"She is always complaining that she does all the work while Mary does none of it," said her mother after Martha had stormed away and renewed her heavy-footed assault on the stairs leading down to the living quarters. "Mary does her share, she just thinks different than Martha."

"I wish Miriam would be so industrious to help out, even if I had to listen to the complaining," said Mary. "With both sets of twins, it gets very tiring at times. I could certainly use the help. What did you do to get Martha to 'want' to do house chores?"

"I learned that trick from my mother when I was their age," said the farmer's wife. "Just as I was at Martha's age, I put her in charge of all the cleaning. I have to put up with some attitude from time to time, but I do get a clean house out of it." Both ladies laughed at the remark and Mary stored the information for immediate use on Miriam once she got back to Nazareth.

Matthew and Joseph had stopped their conversation for a short moment as Martha had thrown her fit but were soon back on track. Because both men farmed, they had a common interest, along with both of them having a family. Jesus and Lazarus had gone down to the street almost as soon as the two had taken off their meeting cloaks and paid their respects to their mothers on the roof.

"Okay," said Lazarus as he finished scratching two lines in the dirt on opposite sides of the small town. "This will be the race to decide all the races. No tricks, no rocks in the shoes, just the fastest between us. Deal?"

"Deal," said Jesus with a smile on his face. "But win, lose or tie, we will always be best friends."

"Any time you need a place to stay when you are down in Judea and Jerusalem, you can stay with me," said Lazarus. "This will be my place when my father and mother pass on and my sisters will surely be married off by then."

Both boys toed the line with their dusty sandals. It had been decided that they would go on the count of three.

"One," yelled Lazarus.

"Two," said Jesus, who had bent his head down as his muscles tightened in preparation for the sprint.

"THREE," screamed both boys as they took off in a cloud of dust and dirt. The race ended with both boys crossing the finish line together and collapsing in a heap on the ground. The farm boy had been practicing ever since losing to Jesus the day he had brought him home and now was rewarded with a draw for his hard work.

"How did you get faster?" asked Jesus in gasps as he caught his breath.

"Ever since you beat me that first day I have been running with rocks tied to my belt," said Lazarus who was sitting up and bent over with his head between his legs. "I knew that first day I couldn't beat you without some kind of edge and practice."

Forty-Five

The Road Home

Early the next morning after saying their good-byes, the carpenter's family started on the road back up to Jerusalem. Instead of going back through the city, the three journeyed past the gate that lead to the Temple and past the garden that was opposite it. The road that they were on would lead them to Jericho. From there they would travel the King's Highway straight north, on a parallel track with the Jordan River. Once they came to the Sea of Galilee, they would turn west and head for Nazareth. The road Joseph had chosen was at least one day longer than going through the passes of Samaria, but he thought, safer.

Without the mass of people that made up a caravan, the three of them would be sitting ducks. With the violence that had happened on the way down, Joseph did not want Mary, Jesus, or himself to be the object of revenge for the robbers.

There was another reason for the detour. Elizabeth and John lived in Jericho and Mary had mentioned to Joseph after Passover that she would like to visit her if they had the time. Without the smaller children, Joseph knew that there would be no time like the present for them to visit.

As the three passed a Roman Inn and tavern situated in front of a small, rundown town that had clearly seen better days, Jesus cried out in delight. "This must be the place that the Samaritan brought old Micah," exclaimed Jesus. "Can we stay here for the night, father?"

"Not this trip," said Joseph, looking at the position of the sun. "We have just enough time to get to Jericho before it gets too dark. We have delayed too long as it is." The three travelers pressed on and came to the gates only minutes before the sun went down that evening.

"What business do you have at Jericho?" asked the guard as he leaned on what Jesus thought was a particularly sharp pointed spear. "It's late and I was about to close the gates for the night."

"We are here to see Elizabeth, widow of Zacharias the priest," said Joseph, as he idly massaged his left arm that had pained him for the better part of the day. "She is my wife's kin."

"Come inside quickly then, for I have heard of roving bands about that have come down from the passes of Samaria. They were driven out of the mountains by a passing Roman guard a few days back, after they attacked it thinking that it was a normal caravan," said the town guardsman, who after passing the traveling family through, closed the gates and ordered the watch lamps lit. Turning back to Joseph, who along with Mary and Jesus had stopped just inside the gate, the guard went on.

"Apparently the Romans have taken to dressing like common men and it's rumored, like women, in their attempt to engage the thieves in battle. The thieves have come this way to avoid any more losses to their number."

"We shall have to be more careful as we make our way back up north to the Sea of Galilee," said Joseph to the man and also to Jesus and himself. "Do you know if they are roving that far north?" he asked the guard.

"Don't know as of yet," said the guard. "We were expecting a load of spice from Damascus that is over due now three days. That may be a clue to answer your question."

"Thank you for the information," said Joseph, who made no move to leave. "If I may ask one more question," asked the carpenter with an almost embarrassed look on his face.

"She lives up on the straight street, where it meets the flat walls, at a place we call Rahab's Corner," said the guard who had anticipated the traveling carpenter's question.

Bowing to the man, Joseph said, "Thank you again and may the God of Peace be with you, your family and all who look to you for safety."

Forty-Six

In Search of Soft Targets

Lucius looked around the fire and shook his head in disbelief. The four thieves were sitting on the boxes of spices that had been taken from the spice merchant traveling from Damascus to Jericho. The price for taking those boxes staggered the leader like nothing had before.

A week before Lucius had thought things could not get any worse. The last caravan that he and his gang of 30 men, women, and children had hit had been a Roman decoy trap. That misadventure alone had cost him half of his group. The swords and javelins of the masquerading legionnaires had killed the lucky ones outright. The unlucky ones had been crucified on the spot, their bodies left to die while hanging from the trees that lined the north-south road through the Samaritan Mountain Pass.

Lucius had decided that enough was enough. First his three best men were arrested and taken away by the legionnaires, and then Barabbas's father was fish-hooked by the boat-hook wielding Galilean traveler. Now the Roman army was playing games – deadly games. Ten of the gang led by Lucius decided to move east, toward the Jordan River. The five that were left behind were two of his men's wives and their daughters. They would drift back to their home cities at the base of Mount Gerizim. While the husbands and their sons understood the risks of the life they lived, none of them wanted to think of their women hanging from crosses in agony.

Now as Lucius looked at what was left of his gang, he just hung his head. The spice merchant had taken six of the men he had brought with him to the Jordan valley. Of those, he would have to explain to two of their wives why they were never coming back. The gang now comprised of Lucius, Barabbas, Nidel, and Nidel's son, Sidel. The rest had all been spent when they had attacked the spice dealer and discovered that the man had two guards equipped with the latest steel swords from their home city. Those guards had chopped down six of his club-equipped gang before Barabbas had shot the men full of arrows.

Lucius looked at the orphaned child and smiled. The boy was getting quite good with the bow he had taken from the legionnaire he had killed a week ago. That they were encountering so much violence called for a discussion.

"We need to change our tactics," he said to the lookout and the two boys. "We also need to discuss what we can and can not do. Apparently, the rules have changed."

"I'd say they have," said Nidel with an angry tone in his voice. One of the men who had been hacked up had been his brother-in-law. "Before, we had enough people to stop a large caravan and enough men to intimidate even the most foolhardy and brave."

"Yeah," piped in Sidel. "Now we attack with the element of surprise three men traveling with a wagon and get nearly wiped out."

"So is that it?" asked Barabbas in a quiet voice. "Do we give up and put our tail between our legs like the dogs that the Jews and Romans think we are?"

"No," said Lucius. "But we must be more careful. Until more men can be found to join our ranks we must choose wisely who we hit."

"Why don't I just fill them with arrows first and we can pick through the booty at our leisure?" asked Barabbas. "It would be a lot easier and a lot safer."

"It would also draw the legions to us like bees to honey," said Nidel. "Be careful young Barabbas. Killing can become a habit that will bring you nothing but hate and contempt for everyone, including in the end, ourselves."

The young man started to say something but was cut off by Lucius. "This is how it will be. We will look for single men who are dressed in fine robes traveling alone on the road."

"How about small families?" asked Sidel. "They couldn't put up that much of a fight, could they?"

"Only if they are fewer in number that we are and have only one grown man," answered Lucius. "Stealing and robbing people of their valuables and money is all fine and nice, but remember, we can't enjoy it if we are dead."

Forty-Seven

Targets of Opportunity

Joseph, Mary, and Jesus left Elizabeth and John's house after only staying one full day. Joseph and Mary were starting to worry about the rest of their children and also the crops that they had in the field. Joseph also knew that he probably had quite a bit of carpentry work waiting for him.

"So when do you think you will leave for the wilderness?" asked Jesus to his cousin, whom he felt he had known forever.

"I must first make sure my mother is well cared for," answered John. "The Lord will tell me and show me when it is time."

"Take care," said Jesus. "I've heard more than one story about how dangerous it is out there."

"You should be the one to say that, after what you went through on the way to Jerusalem," laughed John. "God has a plan for you, Jesus. He will not let anything get in the way of that plan, I'm sure."

Joseph once again thanked the city guard who had been helpful and kind the day before when they had arrived as his family passed through the gate. "Any new reports of the bandits?" asked Joseph.

"Not since I talked to you last night," answered the guard with a smile on his face that quickly evaporated at a thought. "The spice merchant never showed up. It's like he vanished or maybe he took a different route."

The family left very early, at first light. It had been many years since Joseph had taken the Jordan River Road, also known by its ancient name of the King's Highway but he knew that the longest leg of the journey for he and his family would come today. The three Nazarene citizens would have to travel without stopping even for food if they were to make it to Salim before nightfall. That city was just to the south of the Sea of Galilee and from there they would only be two days' journey getting home.

While the Romans had been very good at building their inns on every major road in their empire, they did not consider the Jordan road to be of any military significance and had ignored the stretch of dirt road between the Dead Sea and the Sea of Galilee. With no safe haven between the two cities, the family had no other choice but to try and make it to Salim before the night turned to black.

Soon they had crested a hill and walked down into the Jordan Valley wilderness. They could see the Jordan River off to their right as they made their way north. Looking back just once, Jesus saw the city of Jericho sitting up on the hill, looking down on the plains. From his angle he could clearly see the stones that littered the hills around the city. He remembered the story of General Joshua and that very city. The stones, he thought, must be the fallen walls.

With a prayer of thanksgiving for the miracles that God had provided in the past, Jesus turned his face toward the north and picked up his pace. His parents were already a little out in front of him and he wanted to catch up.

At noon, the family stopped to eat and refresh themselves at the river. At this point, the road ran right alongside of the muddy water. By being very careful not to disturb the bottom, they were able to skim water from the top of the running stream that was clean to drink and wash with. The stop lasted only ten minutes and then Joseph motioned his wife and son that they needed to move along. The family had come halfway to their destination but would still be fighting the darkness before they arrived in Salim.

About an hour later, they came across an abandoned wagon, sitting off the side of the road with no animal attached. The family was surprised to see signs of life. They had not seen anyone on the road since they had left that morning coming or going in either direction.

Upon further inspection, they discovered that the wagon had held spices and that no sign of anyone attending it could be found. Joseph mentioned what the guard at the gate of Jericho had told him about the shipment due in from Damascus and figured that this is what had become of it. Inspecting the wood of the wagon with the professional eye of a carpenter, Joseph's eyes narrowed when he saw the steal arrowhead imbedded in the side.

Straightening, suddenly Joseph wanted to be far away from this place. "Let's go," he said to his family. "This was a place of ambush not too many days ago. It may still be watched." With that the family took to the road once more, walking, if possible with greater speed than before.

Nidel watched as the family inspected the wagon and then hurried off. It was a nice touch of Lucius to put it back on the road, he thought. Everyone who passed by stopped to inspect it and gave him the time he needed to give them a thorough once over. They never saw him, of course. He was too quiet and careful and had lived through too many ambushes that had gone bad.

Deciding that this family fit the criteria that had been laid out by the gang a few days before, the lookout gave the signal and then followed along from behind. Because of the loss of manpower caused by the depletion of the gang's ranks, he now had to help out in the raids along with his primary duty of spotting unsuspecting marks.

The three figures appeared on the road in front of the carpenter and his family as if they had materialized out of thin air. Joseph stopped when he saw whom it was that he faced.

Lucius likewise, was in shock when he saw who it was that confronted him. His ears still ringed from the blow the man in front of him had given him and sometimes, his head ached and his brain felt like it was loose inside his head.

Jesus jumped when he heard a scratch on the road from behind him and when he turned in that direction saw Nidel coming up slowly from the rear.

"Stay calm," said Joseph, whose face was quickly turning red from the pasty white it had been just seconds before. "What do you want?" Joseph asked the man who had hit Miriam.

"Oh come now, friends," said Lucius. "You know very well what it is that I want. The question is whether we'll take it from you while you're alive or when you're dead." As the leader of the thieves mentioned death, Barabbas lifted up his bow and drew an arrow. He pointed the business end toward the trapped family and smiled. Turning toward Lucius, the murdering young man said, "This is how it's supposed to happen."

Joseph looked at his son and at his wife and knew they would have to give over to the thieves what little money they had. It irked the Nazarene carpenter that he and his boy didn't have some of the tools of their trade with them. Then he thought of how very blessed they might be that they didn't. Looking at the boy drawing the bow at them, Joseph could see that the boy had killed before and was anxious to do so again.

"All I have is in this pouch," said Joseph to Lucius as the latter came up to the family. "Giving it to you can't be any worse than giving it to the tax collector."

"Giving all the valuables you have to me is the only way to save your lives," said Sidel as he looked at Jesus. "Feeling a little less brave without your big hammer?"

"Why don't you just take what you've come to steal and be away," said Jesus. "We still have a long journey before night falls."

"I will take the pouch, not that it is all that heavy," said Lucius as he reached out took the money pouch from Joseph's belt. Turning to Jesus he said, "You wouldn't hold out on me now would you boy?"

"I doubt that I have anything that would interest you," said Jesus. "I will pray for you, however, that the Lord God would change your hearts."

"Ha," cried Lucius as the rest of the gang also fell into laughter. Barabbas came up and spit into the carpenter's apprentice's face. "The last thing I want from you or any other Jew is your prayers," said the hateful young man.

"We must be going now," said Nidel, who was ever conscious of the time. Mary had not said a word, but had turned and was watching the lookout man while her husband and son dealt with the three that blocked the road.

"Indeed we do," said Lucius. "Before I go, however, I have something to give to this man." Before Joseph could move or defend himself, Lucius lashed out with a cruel kick that caught the carpenter in the stomach. "That is for the ringing in my ears that I still hear ever night while I sleep." As he spoke, the highwayman brought his club down on the head of Joseph, who had doubled over in pain. "And that is for the terrible headaches that keep me from sleeping at night."

The carpenter hit the ground and did not move. Jesus cradled his father's head in his lap as he watch the robbers melt back into the landscape. He could still hear their laughter when Mary reached her men and started to cry.

Forty-Eight

Something Terribly Wrong

Joseph regained consciousness about ten minutes after the thieves left. His head felt on fire and he groaned as the pain in his head matched the throbbing pain in his stomach.

"How do you feel?" asked Mary who looked at the man she loved with grave concern.

"Ah neeeeeth sooo wather," said Joseph, his speech slurred to the point that both Jesus and Mary had to ask him three times to repeat what he said.

After drinking about half the water that the family had kept in a pouch, Joseph felt strong enough to stand up. His left arm seemed not able to support his weight and he motioned to Jesus to help him stand. Taking him by the left arm while the carpenter used his right hand to push off from the ground, the beaten man stood shakily to his feet.

"We need to go before it gets dark," said Joseph, who had to repeat this sentence five times before he finally started to limp down the road waiving for his family to follow. Jesus and Mary followed the hurt man and both started to pray. They had seen people beat down before, and while the person usually had a severe headache when they woke up, they could usually function all right.

As the family walked throughout the day, usually with Jesus holding Joseph up, it became increasingly clear that Joseph suffered from more than just a hit on the head. The

Nazarene man had no feeling in the whole left part of his body and his speech was still slurred. After a few hours of walking and stumbling, his eyes started to clear from the cloudy and glassy look that they had.

Two hours after the sun had set; the three stumbled into the city of Salim. After pounding on the city's gates for what seemed like forever to Jesus, the night watchman had finally come and upon questioning and calling for backup, had let the family into the city. Mary, remembering something from the search for Jesus in Jerusalem, asked for directions to the town's carpenter.

"Why do you need to see him?" asked the guard. "You don't have a wagon or anything else with you that he could fix do you?"

"My husband here is the carpenter in Nazareth," explained Mary to the suspicious guard. "We were robbed and he was beaten. Something is wrong with him and we need a place to stay. I thought maybe the town's carpenter would take us in."

The guard eyed the three dirty and downtrodden travelers more closely. The man, who was sitting on the ground, had not said a word and now that the guard looked at him, he did indeed see the massive bruising on his head

"I should have seen his condition before," said the guard who now started giving directions to the men he had called for backup. "Go get Lukas, the town physician, and send him to Jacob's place. Tell him it's an emergency, that a traveler has been robbed and beaten."

Turning back to Mary the guard said, "Jacob is the town's carpenter. I bet he would take all of you in, seeing that your husband is a carpenter. I've called for the town's doctor to meet us there."

With that, the guard helped Jesus lift Joseph off the ground. Once the hurt man was standing, the guard led the way to the home of Jacob while Jesus nearly carried his bigger father. One of the other guard's helpers had ran ahead to the town's carpenter's house and had alerted him to his coming guest.

"Oh my goodness, it's Joseph," were the first words out of Jacob's mouth when he saw the travelers approach. "Lydia," he cried to his wife, "come help these people. I know him."

Forty-Nine

Recovery

"I can't tell you why he can't speak properly," said the Greek physician Lukas. "And I have no idea why he has lost all the feeling on the left side of his body."

"Did the blow to his head cause all of this?" asked Mary as Jesus and Jacob looked on. "He was also viciously kicked in the stomach."

"I've seen men beaten before, but this seems like something different," said Lukas as he picked up Joseph's right hand and pressed two of his fingers into his patient's wrist. "From the way the rhythm of his heart is, which is very fast, I would say that this is something unrelated to the beating he sustained. The beating didn't help, that is for sure. But I doubt it was the cause."

"May I ask a few questions of the two of you?" asked the Greek doctor finally looking up at his charges relatives. "Have you ever noticed him getting out of breath easily? Does his face turn bright red when he is upset?

"Yes to both," said both wife and son at the same time. "He's always been like that," said Mary. "He just had to stop and breathe deeply for a few minutes and then he would be all right."

"I see," said the doctor, who then stood up and motioned that they should leave the room. Once out in the main room of Jacob's home, the doctor started to speak again. "I have seen this before, when I was studying medicine in Athens. It seems that the blood of some people boils or gets hot or something and then attacks the brain and other parts of the body. That is why they turn bright red, from the blood. I believe that is what has happened here."

"Will he get better?" asked Mary.

"Sometimes they do and other times not," said the physician with a shrug of his shoulders. "I have seen a complete recovery of the patient and I have seen another such attack occur that kills the one who is suffering. Time will tell with him." With that the physician left the house, saying that he would be back the next day.

Later Jesus sat talking with Jacob while Mary sat beside the bed that held her husband.

"How did you know my father?" asked Jesus. "As far as I know, he never did business this far east or south."

"In truth, now that I think about it, I have seen all three of you before," said the Salim carpenter. "About nine years ago, your father, mother and you came through town. Your father came to me for lodging and asked if he could do any odd jobs in order to pay. He said he was a carpenter like me and that he was on his way to Nazareth where he had some land."

"That must have been when we came back from Egypt," said Jesus. "That was a long time ago."

"There was something about your father and to tell the truth, something about you, that appealed to me. I didn't charge him anything and sent you back on the road with more provision than what you came with," said Jacob. "I've never forgotten him and have always meant to go to Nazareth one of these days to check in on him and his family. I've just never had the time."

"I don't think he can travel any more even if he feels better in the morning," said Jesus. "I think the trip from the place we were robbed to here almost killed him."

"Let me think about that," said Jacob. "If there is something I can do, rest assured young man, I'll do it."

Fifty

Going Home

Joseph was asleep for nearly two days before he awoke. Mary had only left his side for those times when she felt nature's call and when she had to eat. When she did sleep, it was on the ground next to her husband.

The Nazarene carpenter awoke to his wife sponging his bruised forehead with cool water. "What ... day is it?" asked Joseph slowly but clearly, his speech only slurred because of the sleep.

Not answering his question, Mary cried out for Jesus to come to her before she hugged her husband and started to cry. The only thing that Joseph could understand coming out of her mouth was "Thank you God, Thank you God."

"So that's how I ended up here again after so many years?" asked Joseph after listening to Jesus and Mary fill him in on what happened after the beating.

"You don't remember walking the rest of the way to Salim with Jesus and me?" asked Mary.

"All I remember is getting kicked and losing my breath and then my head exploded and that's it," said Joseph. "It was my intention to come to Jacob's house when we got here. I figured if the gates were closed, he would be the only one to speak for us so that they would let inside the city."

"I remembered him once I saw him and he cried out your name when he saw you hurt," said Mary. "I just forgot what town we were in and I was so worried about you, Joseph."

"Well, we have been here several days now," said Joseph who stood with the help of a stick. "It is time that we be leaving and getting home. Zebudee will be wondering what has become of us and he can't ignore his fishing forever."

"Jacob and I have been talking father," said Jesus, looking at his father's face. "He has offered to take us home to Nazareth in his wagon and I have agreed. You are in no position to walk and besides, Lukas the doctor says that any hard exertion will bring on another attack."

"You decided?" asked Joseph with a smile. "You are a man now, aren't you? We'll ride home and let Jacob do the driving."

The trip took two days since the wagon could only go on the main roads and that meant going to Tiberias by the Sea of Galilee before turning west toward Nazareth. Joseph seemed fine the first day and at times walked with his friend and fellow carpenter until he would tire out and rejoin Mary in the wagon. Jesus walked behind the wagon, constantly looking over his shoulder and praying for the safety of his family and newfound friend.

The second day of their travels, after spending the night at an inn in Tiberias, Joseph seemed sick to his stomach most of the morning. He also complained of a massive headache and held his head tightly in both hands while the wagon bounced along the road.

At about mid-day, Mary called out for Jesus to come to her. "He wants to talk to you," was all that she said before climbing off the wagon and running up to where Jacob was leading the ox that was pulling them.

Jesus climbed up on the moving wagon and bent down near Joseph. One look was all that was needed to tell Jesus that he had suffered another attack and that this time he was dying.

"I don't know how long I'll be able to talk and be understood, Jesus, so listen to me carefully," said Joseph when he realized that his eldest son had taken his right hand. "I've lost feeling again on my left side and I can't see anything. It's like someone has closed the shutters from the inside out. Jesus gripped his father's hand as he listened to the man speak.

"I'm not your real father, Jesus," said Joseph with a crooked smile that was caused by the approaching paralysis. "An angel from God came to me when your mother was pregnant with you and told me that you would save the people from their sins. The angel told me what name to call you and he told me to marry your mother. He came back later and told me in a dream to take you away right before Herod the Great had all the boys your age slaughtered."

Joseph rested for a moment before taking a deep breath. "The angel said that you were conceived by the Holy Spirit of God Himself. God has plans for your life that go far beyond being a carpenter in Nazareth and even Israel. Did you know any of this? Has God revealed His plan for your life to you?"

Jesus looked down on his earthly father as tears gathered in his eyes. "I've been sent by the Heavenly Father to carry out His will. What that will is and when I'm to do it, God has not shared with me yet. When the appointed time comes, He will tell me."

"Until that time, you must take my place and take care of the family," said Joseph. "Even if I live through the next attack, I fear I will be not be able to move or speak. Take care of your mother until your brothers are old enough to do so. When they are old enough, then God will reveal His will for you to do."

Jesus hugged Joseph to himself as the tears flowed more freely and splashed down on the unfeeling face of Joseph. The last sentence spoken by the stricken man had been all but intelligible as the paralysis spread over the carpenter's body.

The cart had stopped shortly after Mary had climbed out. She had gone to tell Jacob that Joseph was apparently close to death. The two had witnessed the charge given Jesus and Jacob's eyes had grown large at the mention of how Jesus was conceived.

As Jesus reached out for his mother to come back onto the cart, Joseph suddenly rolled over and vomited. When Mary and Jesus rolled him back onto his back, they could see that he was gone. The first attack had taken his strength and the last had now taken his life.

Jesus looked up to his heavenly Father as he heard his mother start to wail. Jacob's hands took him by the arm and pulled him down from the cart. When he saw his mother grieve, he took her and held her as she sobbed uncontrollably on his shoulder.

Fifty-One

The Carpenter of Nazareth

"Hello, family," said Jesus as he came out of the room he slept in above the shop – for four months, his shop. "Good morning, mother. Did you sleep alright?"

"Good morning, Jesus," said Mary. There were lines on her face and grey in her hair that hadn't been there before Joseph had died. "I didn't sleep all that much, but what I did get was good. What do you have planned for today? Will you be in the shop or out in the fields?" Her voice was quiet and sad. She still grieved for the man she had lost.

"I'll be in the shop most of the day," said Jesus. He turned to look at James, finishing his morning meal in silence. "I will have to go to school this afternoon, though. James, do you want to help me in the shop this morning? I have several jobs waiting and could use another set of hands."

"No," said James quietly as he got up from the family's table and from the cushion he had been reclining on. "I'm going to the fields. I'll try to come back this evening and help you when you get done at the synagogue."

"Fine," said Jesus. who patted his younger brother on the back. "I appreciate the hard work that you are doing."

"James, do you want to take some fruit and figs with you to the field?" asked Mary. Her sons were growing up too fast.

"Not today, thank you," mumbled James as he kissed his mother on the cheek before making his way down the stairs.

"He's not a man yet and he puts in a whole days work," said Mary with both worry and pride evident in her voice. "He has changed so much in the past few months."

"He's very angry with the Samaritans right now," said Jesus, looking at his mother. "I'll do for him what I can, but in the end he will have to take his pain to the Heavenly Father." James had seemed to grow up immediately when he saw his father's body being carried in on Jacob's wagon. He had stopped teasing his sister and now spent most of his days working in the fields, not saying much, not smiling, not laughing. The carpenter saw the grief and burden in his eyes every time they talked.

Jesus knew he would have to watch his brother or, as he had learned from Joseph and confirmed with conversations with his mother, half-brother. While the dead could only be brought back to life in the resurrection, the living had to go on until it was their time to follow. Jesus didn't want James to hold a grudge against the robbers or the Samaritans. That kind of hate would wreck him and ruin his life.

The younger of the two sets of twins ran into the room chasing each other before launching themselves at their mother. "I need to go," said Jesus, receiving a big hug from one of his little sisters. "We'll talk more about James tonight."

"I will see you at noon," said Mary, who had become preoccupied with the swarming twins.

Jesus went down to the workshop that had been Joseph's and his father Jacob's before that. He picked up a piece of wood to start working it, but could not become motivated for the job at hand. Abruptly, he set down the wood gently, left the shop, and walked toward the town gates.

Jesus looked down on the grave of Joseph and smiled. He knew that in the resurrection, he would be reunited with this man who had called him son and hidden both his mother's shame and her miracle. He could not stay long at the grave, for the work had piled up and he had more jobs in the carpentry shop than one man could handle.

Jesus looked toward his Heavenly Father for support and help. It did not seem fair that he would have to be the head of his family at the age of twelve and at times the load was more than he thought he would be able bear. Then bowing his head and submitting to the will of the Creator, Jesus prayed, "Not my will, but Your will be done."